Things
Could Be Worse

Lily Brett was born in Germany and came to Melbourne with her parents in 1948. Her first book, *The Auschwitz Poems*, won the 1987 Victorian Premier's Award for poetry, and was short-listed for the *Age* Book of the Year and Braille Book of the Year. In 1986 her sequence of poems 'Poland' won the Mattara Poetry Prize. Her second book, *Poland and other poems*, was published in 1987, and her third, *After the War*, is being published concurrently with this volume. *Things Could Be Worse* is her first collection of fiction. Lily Brett is married to David Rankin; they live in Melbourne with their three children.

David Rankin is a prominent Australian painter, represented in most major collections and winner of many Australian art prizes, including the 1983 Wynne Prize. He was born in the UK and came to Australia with his family in 1948.

Things Could Be Worse

LILY BRETT

ILLUSTRATIONS BY DAVID RANKIN

MEANJIN / MELBOURNE UNIVERSITY PRESS
1990

First published 1990
Printed in Australia by
Brown Prior Anderson Pty Ltd, Burwood, Victoria, for
Meanjin, and Melbourne University Press, Carlton, Victoria 3053

National Library of Australia Cataloguing-in-Publication entry

Brett, Lily, 1946– .
Things could be worse.
ISBN 0 522 84414 6 (cloth).
        0 522 84426 X (paper).

I. Rankin, David, 1946– . II. Title.
III. Title: Meanjin.

A823.3

For Patricia Kenwood

ACKNOWLEDGEMENTS

Some of these stories have appeared in different forms in the following publications: *Overland*, the *Canberra Times*, *Meanjin*, *Island* and *Australian Short Stories*

Contents

It Was After The War

It was only after the war that Renia Bensky became obsessed with death.

In Germany in 1945, Renia had contemplated suicide. Her baby son was dead. Her mother and father were dead. Her grandparents were dead. Her brothers and sisters were dead. Her aunts and uncles and nephews and nieces were dead. Everybody she had belonged to was dead.

Her girlfriend, Basia, after surviving Stuthof and Auschwitz, had thrown herself off the top of a five-storey building. But Renia Bensky was too tired to die.

She sat in the barracks of the displaced persons camp and sewed. A British soldier had given her part of an old parachute. Renia was making a blouse for herself and a skirt for Rooshka, the young girl in the next bunk.

Rooshka screamed for her mother every night. As soon as Rooshka began, Renia would run out of the barracks with her hands clamped over her mouth. She was frightened her own screams would fly out.

The rhythm of the stitching reassured Renia. The skirt was taking shape. Some things were still predictable.

Renia didn't know where her husband was. She had been separated from Josl when they arrived in Auschwitz. She learnt later that he had been sent to a labour camp. Lists of the dead and the living were posted up regularly in the DP camp. Every day, Renia read the lists. But Josl's name had

1

not yet appeared. Renia didn't know if Josl was alive. She didn't know if she was alive.

Renia was suffering from a bad cold the day she found out that Josl had survived. She hadn't had a cold in her whole year in Auschwitz. Nobody had had a cold. There had been plenty of typhoid, and the Gestapo recorded diseases among the prisoners that had previously been seen by the SS doctors only in medical textbooks. But there were no cases of the common cold. Now Renia's nose dripped, her voice was hoarse and she had a harsh cough.

She could hardly look at Josl when they met. She felt separated from him by what she had seen, and what she had breathed. She felt poisoned. She could hardly accept who she was now. Her new knowledge was embedded in her. It seeped through her every thought. Sometimes it attacked her in her sleep and she would wake up crying. She knew it would always be like this.

How could she embrace Josl? How could she let him embrace her? She was not Renia Bensky, wife of Josl Bensky. She was someone else. She was a stranger to Josl. She was a stranger to herself.

Josl looked almost the same as when she had last seen him. He was much thinner, but he had the same childlike, optimistic smile that used to make her want to cry. He looked at her quietly for a few minutes. Renia now saw that he looked exhausted. He kissed her on the cheek.

In Auschwitz the prisoners were pressed so closely together on the bunks that they could only turn over if the whole row turned together. Often prisoners' vomit or diarrhoea dripped through the bunks.

In Germany after the war, when Renia watched Jewish girls flirting with soldiers, she wondered how they could think that there was any comfort to be had from somebody else's body.

When Renia kissed Josl, he wept. She knew that he understood something. She didn't know what. She went to her barracks and vomited and vomited. Josl sat silently and watched her vomit.

When she arrived in Australia in 1948, Renia Bensky hated it. Melbourne was so empty. And the food! The cheese tasted like wax, and the bread was like cotton wool. The people at the Jewish Welfare Agency were kind. They found the Benskys a room in Brunswick, and gave them a bed, four blankets and two pillows. But Renia felt so alone. More alone than she'd felt in Auschwitz. More alone than she'd felt in the ghetto.

Renia and Josl were taken out by Josl's cousin, Max Borg, who had come to Australia in 1933. Max's friends, who were mostly assimilated Jews, looked at Josl and Renia strangely. Renia felt that she was an embarrassment to Max's wife, Esther.

Max and Esther were lesser lights in the Jewish social life of Melbourne. Renia could see that Esther looked down on her. One of the first things Esther had said to Renia was: 'You should buy yourself an Australian dress. Here it is called a sunfrock. It will help you look like an Australian. We Jews are just beginning to be accepted, and you shouldn't cause trouble for us. Last week the bank manager did come to us, to our house, for a cup of coffee. He had coffee and a piece of cake, and he saw that we are normal, just like everybody else. It is important to be normal.'

Josl tried to tell Max what had happened to Max's niece in Poland, but Max stopped him. 'I know, Josl, she had a terrible time. You know, Josl, we didn't have it so easy here in Melbourne during the war. We couldn't get any herring. It wasn't so easy.'

Renia tried once to talk to Frieda. Frieda was the nicest of Esther's friends. Frieda had taught Renia to make gefilte fish, and she always talked to Renia with tenderness in her voice. 'Frieda, do you know that I saw some terrible things in Poland,' Renia said one day. 'In concentration camp, I wanted to keep living so I could tell somebody what I saw.'

Frieda interrupted her. 'Renia darling, it is over now. You are here, safe in Australia. It is best to put those things out of your mind. It is best not to disturb yourself with those thoughts.'

Esther's daughter, twelve-year-old Rivka, once asked Josl why he had big holes in his back. Renia and Josl were at St Kilda beach with the Borg family. Josl began to answer. 'It was . . .' he began. Esther grabbed Rivka by the arm with such ferocity that the girl began to cry. She dragged Rivka away. Fragments of Esther's conversation with Rivka floated over the tea-trees. 'He could have a heart attack if he talks about such things. You should know better.' Rivka returned red-faced and swollen-eyed.

After one month in Australia, Renia wanted to leave. But she had nowhere to go to. She remembered how she had begged Josl to get them out of Germany. From the moment Josl and Renia were reunited, all Renia's thoughts were focused on leaving Europe. She hated Germany. Every German sounded like a Kommandant. Josl gave her ten American dollars for her twenty-third birthday. With her birthday money, Renia bought four extra locks for the door of the room they were renting in Bayreuth. When Renia found out that she was pregnant, she bought another two locks.

One morning Renia was alone in the room. She was stitching the edges of a square of woollen material to make a blanket for the baby. The baby was due in one month. At a quarter past ten there was a soft knock at the door. Renia silently walked to the cupboard next to the bed. She got in and closed the cupboard door behind her. When Josl came home at half past six, Renia was still sitting in the bottom of the cupboard.

Josl would have been happy to stay in Germany. For a while, at least. He was doing business on the black market and making a little money. With his first bit of profit he bought Renia a black leather jacket. He felt so proud when he looked at Renia in her new jacket. It was a moment of pure joy. Josl thought that there couldn't be many higher levels of happiness than the happiness he felt looking at Renia in her leather jacket.

The rations that Josl and Renia received in Germany were enough to keep them from starving, but not enough to stop them being hungry. Josl began looking for ways to make more money.

He felt alive. He was no longer tired. He had a beautiful wife, and a child on the way. He had something to live for. God had given him a second chance. Nothing could stop him now.

Josl discovered a supply of extra food. The US army base. Josl waited outside the mess hall. When the soldiers had finished their meals, they scraped their plates into a large rubbish bin. Josl took the best scraps from the bin. He took potatoes, carrots, sausages. Sometimes he was lucky enough to find eggs. The food was so tasty. He carried it home, trimmed some of the chewed edges, and arranged the food nicely on plates. Josl never told Renia where this bounty came from.

Josl's business dealings with the US base expanded. He began buying cigarettes from the soldiers. He sold the cigarettes at a substantial profit. Josl used this profit to buy more cigarettes, and then some tea and coffee and chocolates.

He decided to branch out further. He hid himself on a freight train going to Pilsen in Czechoslovakia. There he did some shopping. He invested the bulk of his money in small electric hotplates.

Josl sold the hotplates to the Americans for cigarettes. He sold the cigarettes to Germans, who paid for them in Allied Marks. Josl sold the Allied Marks to the Americans for US dollars.

He bought an Opel Kadet. It was black, snub-nosed and very shiny. Josl hadn't driven a car for six years. He thought he would burst with pride when he first drove Renia around Bayreuth.

He bought a small white fur coat for baby Lola. This coat would keep her warm in the coldest winter. And he bought a small diamond for Renia. A new engagement ring. A new engagement with the future.

One day Josl was stopped by an American military policeman. The military police, Josl always told Renia, were gangsters, not normal people. 'You just have to look at them and you can see they are not normal,' he would say. 'What normal person wants to be a military police? And they are all so big. Big gangsters. Big criminals. That's what they are.'

The military policeman accused Josl of driving over the speed limit. The Kadet didn't go over sixty kilometres an hour, but Josl didn't argue. He was wondering what he would have to pay this giant to avoid being charged with speeding when the MP ordered him out of the car.

Josl knew he was done for. It took the MP two minutes to find the kilo and a half of butter that Josl had hidden in a box of old papers. Grinning with delight, the MP said 'Today I am in a particularly good mood. If you eat this butter up now, in front of me, you can go home a free man. I will not report you for trading on the black market.' Josl ate the butter. He was sick for a week afterwards.

Every day Renia asked Josl when they could leave Germany. She begged him not to do business on the black market. Each time Josl travelled to Czechoslovakia, Renia prepared herself for news of his death.

Finally, Josl couldn't bear to keep Renia in Germany any longer. They packed up. Josl gave his business tips to his old friend Moishe Mittelman, and Renia, Josl and Lola set off for Australia.

Moishe Mittelman remained in Bayreuth for another three years. In 1951 he migrated to America. He arrived in New York with $50,000.

Soon Renia Bensky became acclimatized to Australia. She no longer felt blinded by the harsh light. She owned sunfrocks and sunglasses. In the summer of 1948 she bought a pair of bathers.

Renia's next-door neighbour, Mrs Brown, taught her how to make an apple pie, and soon Renia's apple pies were the toast of many Sunday card evenings.

Renia became patriotically Australian. She hummed 'God Save The King', and wouldn't let anyone voice any criticism of the country or its people.

Renia began to feel happy. At the same time, a new feeling edged its way to her consciousness. She felt that she was going to die.

In bed at night, Renia began to feel small pains in her chest. She went to see Dr Johnson. He examined her and sent her to the Women's Hospital for tests. 'There is nothing wrong with you,' he told Renia. 'I think, Mrs Bensky, it's your nerves. It is definitely not your heart. Why don't you relax a bit? Do you have a dog? I find that taking the dog for a walk takes my mind off things. Why don't you get a dog?'

Then Renia's periods became irregular. In Auschwitz, Renia had been grateful that her periods had stopped. Her first and only period there had left her with blood-streaked legs and feet. Now, Renia was sure that this irregularity was a symptom of something terminal. Dr Horowitz was kind to her. 'Mrs Bensky,' he said, 'we usually only worry when women bleed too much. Irregular and slight periods are nothing to worry about.' Renia's next period was so heavy and painful that it reminded her of her adolescence.

Renia began to diagnose and prescribe remedies for herself. Her bathroom cupboards contained antibiotics, antihistamines, diuretics, tranquillizers and sedatives. She lectured friends on the difference between a viral and a bacterial infection, and sometimes dispensed medicines to them.

'I won't live long. You won't have me forever,' Renia

used to say to Lola. Sometimes she screamed at Lola: 'You are killing me. Hitler didn't manage to kill me, so you want to finish me off. You will cry on my grave.'

Renia went to a lot of funerals. She went to the funerals of people she hardly knew. She went to the minyans. She looked after the bereaved. But it was not enough. Renia couldn't feel as though she had buried her dead.

During the day, Renia was not alone. She carried the cries of orphans in the ghetto, and demented mothers, and lost fathers. At night when she went to bed all the dead came to visit her. The dead were all unburied. They were all in limbo. Renia often screamed in her sleep. Her screams were the screams of dying Jews. The screams had left the bodies of the dead and lodged themselves in Renia Bensky.

At lunchtime at the Renee of Rome factory, the machinists ate in the staff kitchen. They shared cups of tea, sandwiches, sadnesses and happiness. Renia liked the women. All the sewing machines were pushed together in one corner of the factory, and Renia felt snug sewing in the middle of that crowd of machines. But at lunchtime Renia stood out in the hallway, in the dark corridor on the fourth floor, in Flinders Lane, Melbourne, Australia, and talked to her mother.

'Where are you, Mama? Are you in the air here in Australia? Or did you stay in Poland? I am frightened, Mama, that one day I won't be able to remember your face. Mama, there are no photographs. No photographs of you and Papa. No photographs of Shimek and Abramek, Jacob or Felek. No photographs of Bluma or Fela or Marilla. I tried to go with you, Mama, but somebody knocked me on the head and pushed me into the other line. The line of life, Mama. I don't know if you saw, Mama, I don't know if you knew that I didn't want to leave you. Oh, Mama, I am so lonely.'

Sometimes some of the younger girls at Renee of Rome complained about their mothers. This one's mother didn't understand her, and that one's mother was unfair. Renia used to block her ears and plan what she would cook for dinner.

Renia often said to Lola, 'You don't know how lucky you are to have parents.' And Lola didn't know.

After a few years in Australia, Josl had his own small clothing business. Josl and Renia also had another daughter, Lina. Lina was born with one leg shorter than the other. Renia felt responsible for this. She thought that it could have been due to the fact that she had been bent over a sewing machine eighteen hours a day through the pregnancy. She felt consumed with guilt. She stopped working and stayed at home with Lina. At home, Renia washed and cooked and cleaned and looked after Lina.

She had a beautiful garden. A garden with rose trees and apple trees and lemon trees. Renia loved her garden. Early every morning Renia went outside and fed the birds in the garden. There had been no birds in Auschwitz, and no birds in the ghetto. For six years Renia hadn't seen a bird. Now, about a hundred birds waited for Renia every morning. There were seagulls, sparrows, starlings, willy wagtails and sometimes pigeons.

Renia never went shopping with her friends. She never went to charity luncheons or to fashion parades. She didn't play cards or bridge. She belonged to no clubs. Renia sunbaked.

On sunny days, Renia did her housework faster than usual. She then took the telephone off the hook. She rubbed Nivea cream over her face and her shoulders, and she lay down in the garden in the sun.

Even if it had been raining and the grass was damp, Renia didn't lie on a towel or a beach mat. She lay on the grass.

She loved to feel the earth on her legs, on her hair, on her scalp, on her hands. Lying there, blended into the earth, Renia Bensky felt happy.

Loti Luftman's Daughter

When she arrived in Australia, ten-year-old Michelle Luftman was put into grade one. 'When her English improves we will move her up,' the headmaster said to Esther Borg, Michelle's guardian.

'Mister Herbert,' said Esther Borg, 'Herr Professor, this girl is very clever. She can speak French. She travelled on a boat by herself for eleven weeks to come to Australia. She sat at the captain's table every night. She organized it herself. She had no-one else to organize anything for her. You know that she is an orphan. Herr Professor, if a girl is so clever that she sits at the captain's table, don't you think she doesn't deserve to be in a class with five-year-olds? Don't you think you could put her with children of her own age?' 'All in good time, Mrs Borg. All in good time,' said Mr Herbert.

'It's lucky my Rivka learns French at school,' Esther Borg said to Ada Small, who could speak French, 'and it's lucky I have got you, Ada, to help me, because, to tell you the truth, I don't know what I would do with Michelle otherwise. At least she eats everything that I give her. That you can say about her for sure, she is a very good eater, but she is a bit wild. I am used to my Rivka. She is such a good girl. She studies hard. She doesn't give me any trouble. This one, this Michelle, if I ask her not to dip her bread into her milk, she says "Why?" I tell her it's not nice. But she doesn't care to be nice. She just keeps on putting her bread into her milk. And I know she can understand what I am saying. Oy, Ada, what am I going to do? You think God thought I didn't have enough troubles already?'

Michelle Luftman was the daughter of Esther's third cousin, Loti Luftman. 'I wonder if she has got some of her father's bad blood,' Esther said to Ada Small. 'You know, Ada, Loti married a bad type. He was a gambler with a big eye for the girls. Loti's parents didn't give their blessings to the marriage. This did upset Loti, but she was so madly in love with this gambler that nothing else mattered. They left Lodz in 1937 to live in Paris. I heard that Loti's mother was never the same after her daughter left.'

When Esther was asked by the Jewish Welfare Agency whether she was willing to take in her cousin's daughter, she was horrified. She'd hardly known Loti, so why would they ask her to take in Loti's child? Mrs Silberman from the Jewish Welfare Agency had explained to Esther that welfare agencies in Paris were looking for orphaned Jewish children who had been in hiding during the war or who had lived as Christians in Christian families. They were reclaiming these children and placing them with Jewish families.

Esther was superstitious. She was frightened of not doing the right thing. She reminded herself that it was the greatest honour, in God's eyes, to look after an orphan. And so Esther had said yes, she would take Michelle into her home.

Sometimes, at night, Esther wondered how Loti had died. She knew that she had died in Auschwitz. She knew that by the time Michelle was born the gambler had already left Loti for a wealthy French woman. Esther had heard this news from her cousin in Lodz. Esther had also heard that in 1939 Loti had wanted to come home to Lodz with the baby, but her father had told her that things were very bad in Poland and that she and the baby would be safer in Paris.

Loti was making arrangements to leave for Grenoble

when the Gestapo began rounding up the Jews in Paris. Loti knew that the Gestapo were making surprise raids on Jewish homes. Each time Loti returned to her apartment she left the baby in her pram in the street while she checked the apartment. Inside the pram Loti kept a note. It read: 'This baby is not to be moved until I return. I have only gone inside for a short while.'

The day that the Gestapo were waiting for Loti, she had parked Michelle outside Monsieur Renard's bakery. Monsieur Renard knew Loti and always kept an eye on the pram. Monsieur Renard watched the Gestapo take Loti away. She didn't even glance in the direction of the pram. When Loti hadn't returned by the time it was dark, Monsieur Renard wheeled the pram to his sister's house. He asked his sister to look after the baby until Loti's return. Monsieur Renard's sister kept Michelle for a few days before giving her back to Monsieur Renard. 'She looks too Jewish,' she said to her brother. 'I'm not going to be killed or run the risk of my family being killed for one small Jewish child.'

Monsieur Renard, a middle-aged bachelor, was heart-broken. Michelle was such a sweet child. She could already say a few words, and she was always in a good mood, always smiling. She didn't look Jewish. With her blonde hair and heart-shaped face, she looked more Norwegian than Jewish. But his sister would not change her mind.

Monsieur Renard took Michelle home with him. He kept her hidden in the back of the bakery. Several times a day he would step out of the shop to see if he could see any sign of Loti coming back. After four months Monsieur Renard knew that he had to make a decision about Michelle. Although she was an obedient child, and kept very quiet while the shop was open, it was becoming more and more difficult to hide her. Once, when he hadn't been able to pop into the back and see her for a few hours, she ran into the shop and hugged him.

She was his cousin's child, he explained to a curious

customer, and he was looking after her while his poor cousin recovered from tuberculosis.

But he was nervous. There were many Nazi collaborators, and it was impossible to recognize them. Monsieur Renard's sister heard of a Catholic woman who would take Michelle in, for a small fee. 'Just until her mother comes back. Just until after the war,' Monsieur Renard said to Madame Guillaume. Michelle screamed and screamed when Monsieur and Madame Guillaume came to the bakery to collect her. She clung to Monsieur Renard. It took both men to disengage Michelle from Monsieur Renard. After Monsieur and Madame Guillaume left with Michelle, Monsieur Renard howled like a child.

Michelle stayed with the Guillaume family for eight years. Pierre and Marie Guillaume were good to Michelle. They took her to church every Sunday. She was a curious child, and a quick learner. By the time she was three she could recite the rosary. Several times a day she would say 'Hail Mary full of grace the Lord is with thee. Blessed art thou amongst women and blessed is the fruit of thy womb, Jesus.' She would, if she was asked, say that her mother was Jeanne Lafitte, cousin of Monsieur Renard. 'My mother is very sick in a sanatorium,' she would say.

Monsieur Renard sent a small weekly stipend to Madame Guillaume, but he never came to visit Michelle. A visit, he thought, would disturb her. It would do her more harm than good.

When Michelle was six, Madame Guillaume gave birth to twin boys, Alain and Auguste. Michelle doted on them. She fed them, she sang to them, and she walked them round and round the square in their big double pram.

'I don't know how I would have managed without Michelle. She is a gift to me from God,' Madame Guillaume said to her husband. When the war ended, Madame Guillaume became very agitated. Every day she ran down to the letterbox to see if there was any news of Loti Luftman.

One day a letter arrived from Monsieur Renard. Loti Luftman had perished in Auschwitz, he said. Madame Guillaume could not contain herself. She wept with relief. She did not want to experience her happiness at the expense of somebody else, she told the priest at confession, but she was overjoyed that Michelle was now hers.

On the other side of Paris, Monsieur Renard's sister was bothered by her conscience. Finally, she phoned the Jewish Welfare. 'I have to do this,' she said to her husband. 'I have to make sure that that poor little girl knows who her real people are. I deserted her once, and I am not going to desert her again. It is not right that she is being brought up as a Catholic.'

The day that the people from the Jewish Welfare came to collect Michelle, the whole Guillaume family was crying. Michelle clung to Madame Guillaume. 'Maman, maman, don't let them take me,' she screamed. 'Maman, maman, don't let them take me!'

Mrs Polonsky from the Jewish Welfare escorted Michelle on the train to Marseilles. 'This woman is taking me away from my mother,' Michelle told everyone in the carriage. She repeated it whenever anyone walked through. Nobody took any notice. When Mrs Polonsky tried to put her arm around Michelle, Michelle bit her. When they reached Marseilles, Mrs Polonsky put Michelle on board the boat for Australia. The purser agreed that it would be best if they locked Michelle in her cabin until the boat was ready to leave. When the boat sailed Mrs Polonsky heaved a sigh of relief.

To celebrate Michelle's first birthday in Australia, the Borg family went out to dinner at Giuseppe Botticelli's Italian Cuisine Restaurant in the city.

'Have you got a French onion soup?' Esther Borg asked the waiter.

'We have a beautiful minestrone, but madame, if you wish, we will make you a French onion soup,' said the waiter.

'Good,' said Esther. 'This girl is French, from France you understand, and she likes an onion soup.'

'Excuse me, this is not onion soup,' Esther announced when the soup arrived. 'This is kapushniak.'

'Madame, I assure you that this is French onion soup,' said the waiter.

'This is kapushniak. Polish cabbage soup. And it is not such a good kapushniak,' said Esther.

'You expect an Italian to make a good kapushniak? You are crazy,' said Josl Bensky. The Borgs had invited the Benskys to join the celebration.

'You have to be very careful about what you eat in a restaurant,' said Renia Bensky.

'Yes,' said Josl. 'I did eat some worms last week and oy Gott was I sick. Sick like a dog. I usually don't eat those worms, but they were in a special dish a girl did bring to the factory for her birthday.'

'Josl, they are not called worms,' said Renia. 'They are called prawns.'

'You are, like always, right, Renia, they are called prunes,' said Josl.

'Prawns, Josl, not prunes,' said Renia.

'Prunes and prawns. Sounds like the same thing to me,' said Josl.

'Josl, you have to learn to say the right word,' said Esther. 'We are in Australia and in Australia we speak English. Oy, look who is at the table in the corner. It's Mr and Mrs Belgiorno from the fruit shop. Good evening, Mr and Mrs Belgiorno. Good evening.' Esther lowered her voice: 'She is eating crapes. Crapes is a fish with a shell. It is not trayfe, but maybe one day we will try a crape. After all, none of us is religious.'

'It's not a crape, Mum,' said Rivka. 'It's a lobster.'

'It's for sure not a lobster, it's a crape,' said Esther.

'I think Esther means a crab, not a crape,' said Max Borg.

'Oh. I know what Mum meant,' said Rivka. 'She meant a crayfish.'

'That is what I said, a crapefish,' said Esther.

'It's not for me, such a crapefish,' said Josl.

The next day Max Borg came across Mario Belgiorno in Lygon Street, Carlton.

'How you like that meal last night at Giuseppe Botticelli's?' asked Mr Belgiorno.

'It was very nice,' said Max. 'The kapushniak was not so nice, but I can't complain if an Italian can't make a kapushniak.'

'I had a polenta,' said Mario Belgiorno, 'and this morning I ring Botticelli and I say to him, "Why you put on the menu something you can't cook? I come from Venezia and every Friday we have polenta and fish. You must have a German cook because he put bacon in the polenta." I say to Botticelli, "We don't put bacon in the polenta."'

Max reported this conversation to Esther.

'I knew this restaurant didn't know what they were doing,' she said. 'The kapushniak was shocking.'

When Michelle was twelve, Esther Borg went to see Mr Herbert again. 'Herr Professor,' she said, 'I beg of you to put Michelle into at least grade six. She is a very intelligent girl. So she doesn't want to learn about the grazing lands of Gippsland or the discovery of the Darling or the story of wool, so is this so terrible? What is it about these things that she should be so interested in? Herr Professor, it is something shocking that a twelve-year-old girl should be in grade three. Herr Professor, she is an orphan. Don't you make special allowances for orphans?'

'Mrs Borg, I can see your point of view, but I have a school to run and I can't put a child up who refuses to do her projects,' said Mr Herbert.

Michelle was happy in grade three. She was with the same children she had started school with in grade one. Michelle liked her classmates. She often told them stories about the Guillaume family. The children loved the stories of the twins and how no-one except Michelle could get them to eat beans.

Sometimes, on the way home from school, Michelle would stop at St Kevin's church around the corner from the South Street Primary School. She could still remember her prayers. She never prayed for anything in particular. She was just soothed by the presence of God.

The few times that Michelle mentioned God or the Guillaume family to Esther Borg, Esther would try to stop her from speaking. 'Shush, shush, Michelle,' she would say. 'You mustn't upset yourself. That is in the past, and the past has gone. You are our daughter now and we love you like our own daughter. You must forget the past and think of the future. And better still, you could think of your schoolwork. A girl like you in grade three, it is shocking. Also, you could stop, once and for all, dipping your bread in your milk.'

'I don't know how Esther manages with that Michelle,' said Josl Bensky to Renia. 'This morning Max came to pick me up. He had Michelle in the car. She jumped into the front seat. I said to her: "Excuse me, I am going to sit in the front seat." She said to me: "No, I am. It is my car, not your car." Is that a nice way to behave?'

'You know, Josl, I feel sorry for Michelle,' said Renia. 'She was dragged away from a family who loved her. I hear Esther doesn't even let her write to them. So what, so they were Catholic? She was happy. Is it such an important thing to be Jewish? Look at all the people who died because they were Jewish. Why is it so wonderful to be Jewish? And what sort of a Jew is Esther Borg? Josl, what sort of a Jew is she? Does she go to synagogue? Does she observe even the holiest of holy days? Of course not. So this poor child got dragged from a good family to come and live a Jewish life. Is it such a good life, Josl, that it is better for her?'

Michelle left school at fifteen. She had completed grade five.

'I did my best,' Esther Borg wailed. 'The child wouldn't do her projects. What could I do?'

Max Borg got Michelle a job in the Baumes' grocery shop. Michelle worked there with Mrs Baume and her son, Shmul. Mr Baume worked in a factory. Baume's was the first kosher grocer shop in Melbourne. Michelle weighed and served pickles and herrings. She sliced sausages and packed breads and bottled oil. Sometimes women left their children with Michelle while they went next door to the butcher's.

'Michelle is a wonder with children,' Mrs Baume told everybody, 'and she is a wonder in the shop. I don't know how we managed without her.'

Michelle talked to the customers and she talked to Shmul. She talked to Shmul every day. And Shmul listened. On the eve of Michelle's sixteenth birthday, Shmul asked Michelle to marry him.

'I need this like I need a hole in the head,' Esther Borg said to Max when Shmul asked for Michelle's hand in marriage. 'What for does she want to marry a religious boy? Is this what she came to a modern country to do? To be a religious fanatic? Thank you, no.'

But Max Borg gave the couple his blessing. 'He is a good boy, Esther, and he will be a good husband to Michelle,' said Max.

On their wedding night, Michelle said to Shmul, 'Shmul, maybe if we are very lucky we will have twins.'

'Maybe we will have two sets of twins,' said Shmul.

'You know, Renia, Michelle won't eat at my house any more,' said Esther. 'That's what I needed, a religious maniac. She goes to synagogue, she keeps a kosher house.

My God, she even wears a shaytl, with such beautiful hair, she wears a wig. I said to her last week: "Come on, just take one piece of klops home." She wouldn't. What did I need this for? Soon she won't even have a glass of water in my house. And with that shaytl on she looks like she lives in a village in Poland. I should have been able to see what was happening between her and that Shmul.'

'What you should be able to see, Esther my darling cousin,' said Renia, 'is that Michelle looks happy.'

'Happy, happy, what does Renia Bensky know about happy?' Esther said to Max that night.

'Esther darling, if Michelle won't eat with us maybe you could cook at her house and then everything will be kosher and we can eat there with them?' said Max.

'I have got a shocking headache from being with Renia Bensky, so please leave me in peace,' said Esther.

A year after the wedding, Esther saw Mr Herbert outside the school. 'Hello, hello,' she called to him. 'I would just like to tell you, Herr Professor, that my Michelle has done very well. She has found herself a beautiful husband. He is good to her like gold. And any minute now we are going to be grandparents. And let me tell you, Herr Professor, that she has done all of this without your help. She has done all of this without the projects about the mighty merino or the death of the dinosaur. Yes, Herr Professor, my Michelle has done very well and she has done it all by herself.'

An Illness

Lola Bensky looked at her mother fussing around her younger sister, Lina. Lina had been born with one leg shorter than the other. So what, thought Lola. All it meant was that she limped. But her mother seemed to think it meant Lina's life was in danger.

Mrs Bensky was sitting on Lina's bed. 'Lina darling, it's time to get out of bed and get ready for school. Sit up and drink your orange juice, darling.'

Lola grimaced. She didn't think Lina was a darling.

Lola didn't feel like going to school today. Bruce Matthews had been bothering her in class. Although he was in grade six, he was six feet tall. He had moved into the desk behind Lola. He stuck rude signs on her back, and he looked menacing.

Mrs Bensky was still fussing around Lina. 'Watch her carefully on the way to school, Lola,' she said. 'She can't go without a cardigan.'

'I don't feel well, Mum,' said Lola.

Mrs Bensky looked startled. Lola never got sick. 'You'll feel better after you have something to eat. Your breakfast is on the table,' she said.

Lola knew she would have to try harder if she wanted to stay at home today. 'I feel too sick to eat,' she said.

Mrs Bensky stopped buttoning Lina's cardigan. 'What is wrong with you?' she asked Lola.

'I've got a stomach ache,' Lola said.

Mrs Bensky did look worried now, thought Lola. And no wonder. Lola was always eating. She ate everything that Mrs Bensky fed her and more. She ate so much that Mrs Bensky had to keep all her biscuits, cakes and chocolates locked in the kitchen cupboard.

But Lola knew where the key was. She was an expert at biting off both ends of the walnut horseshoes until they formed smaller horseshoes. She licked the middle of plump, chocolate-filled macaroons, and left them marginally slimmer. She could pick the sultanas and poppyseed out of the strudel and leave it looking untouched.

'Have a nice piece of cantaloup, darling. A piece of fresh cantaloup will make you feel better,' said Mrs Bensky.

This is not working, thought Lola. Maybe Mrs Bensky knew she was lying? Mrs Bensky always said that mothers and policemen could read the truth in children's eyes. Lola kept her eyes averted.

'I think I'm going to vomit,' she said. Nothing happened. Mrs Bensky didn't move. Lola opened her mouth, clutched her stomach, and screamed. Lina started crying. Mrs Bensky rushed to comfort Lina. 'Get into bed, Lola,' she said.

When Lina had calmed down, Mrs Bensky came and sat on Lola's bed. She took Lola's temperature. 'You haven't got a temperature, darling,' she said. 'Maybe it was something that you ate that is giving you the upset stomach? I will take Lina to school and if you are still not feeling well when I come back I will ring Dr Stone.'

Lola was happy. She would spend the day in bed, reading. Mrs Bensky got ready to leave with Lina. Every now and then Lola let out a small groan or a loud whine. Lola felt pleased with herself. Mrs Bensky was starting to look really worried. Lola remembered that there were some fresh almond slices in the cake cupboard. This was going to be a good day.

Mrs Bensky and Lina finally left. Lola leapt out of bed and ran into the kitchen. She had a good fifteen minutes

before Mrs Bensky returned. She grabbed three slices of honey cake, which she had neatly sheared off the sides of larger slices. She took half of a wedge of cheesecake, and boy, was she in luck, there were loose scorched almonds. Her mother would never miss a few handfuls, thought Lola.

Lola hopped back into bed. She ate quickly. That breakfast would have to do her until three o'clock when Mrs Bensky went to pick up Lina.

Lola was swallowing the last scorched almond when Mrs Bensky arrived back.

'Darling, you look a bit red and hot. Where is the pain?' she asked. Lola pointed to the lower part of her stomach.

'Is it still as bad as it was this morning?' said Mrs Bensky.

'It's worse,' said Lola.

'I think I will call Dr Stone,' said Mrs Bensky.

Lola liked Dr Stone. She often chatted to him while he pressed tongue depressants down Lina's throat.

'Dr Stone will be here as soon as he has finished in the surgery,' said Mrs Bensky. She tucked Lola into her bed. 'Are you sure you don't want some cantaloup?' she said.

'No thanks,' said Lola.

'What about an orange juice, freshly squeezed?'

'No thanks, Mum,' said Lola.

Mrs Bensky started to clean the house. Lola settled down with a book under the sheets. From time to time she remembered to moan.

Dr Stone arrived just after lunchtime. Lola had refused to eat any lunch. She was starving. It hadn't been easy to say no to lunch. Mrs Bensky had offered her some apple compote, and some chicken soup with rice. Lola loved chicken soup with rice.

Mrs Bensky had looked very distressed when Lola said no to the chicken soup. Lola started to feel guilty about her mother. Had she taken things too far by refusing the chicken soup?

Dr Stone poked and prodded Lola. He told her to lift her right leg and then to bend it as close to her chest as she could. He asked her to pinpoint the pain in each of these positions. Lola was smart. She was consistent about which part of her stomach hurt most.

When Dr Stone finished, Lola smiled at him, but he wasn't smiling. Dr Stone and Mrs Bensky went into the kitchen. Lola could hear them talking. She was a bit hungry, but on the whole things were working out quite well, she thought. Maybe she would even get to spend another day in bed.

Dr Stone and Mrs Bensky came back into Lola's bedroom. 'Well, my girl,' said Dr Stone, 'I think you have got appendicitis.' Lola felt proud. She looked up at Dr Stone as he continued, 'It seems to be in quite an advanced state. I think we might take you to hospital now.'

Now? Hospital? Lola felt faint. Then she felt sick. Dr Stone helped her to the toilet. She had violent diarrhoea. Dr Stone helped her back to bed. He rang for an ambulance.

Mrs Bensky was weeping. 'Oy, my Lolala, my poor Lolala.'

'I'm going to vomit,' said Lola. Mrs Bensky rushed for a bowl. Lola vomited and vomited.

Lola was still shaking in the ambulance. The ambulance men were very nice. One of them held her hand all the way to St Andrew's Hospital. 'Get a move on,' he shouted to the driver. 'She's in bad shape.'

The nurses were also sympathetic. 'Poor kid, have you eaten anything today?' said a nurse.

'No,' cried Lola.

'Good,' said the nurse. 'Give her a wash,' she said to another nurse, 'and we'll prep her.'

Prep her? What was that? Lola felt sicker and sicker. Her heart raced and she couldn't stop crying. What had happened?

Mr Bensky came rushing in to see his daughter before they wheeled her away. 'Don't worry, darling, you will feel so much better after the operation. My poor darling, you look so terrible. Mum is worried out of her mind. Just remember you will feel much better afterwards,' he said. 'I love you, darling,' he added. Tears ran down Mr Bensky's face as he waved goodbye to Lola.

Afterwards, Lola felt awful. Her throat hurt. She had a horrible ache in her stomach, and her mouth tasted terrible. She wove in and out of a nightmare in which a young nurse kept telling her it was all over and she was fine.

Later, Dr Stone came to see her. 'You have been a very brave girl, Lola,' he said. 'The appendix didn't look too bad. It looked fine actually, but you can never be too safe in these cases. You have got a cut right down the middle of your tummy. We thought we should have a good look around, but all is well in there.'

Lola looked up at him. She knew that he hadn't told her parents and never would.

'Don't worry, you'll be out of hospital in two weeks and we'll get you some ice-cream for that sore throat,' said Dr Stone.

Mr and Mrs Bensky and Lina came to visit Lola. They looked at her solemnly.

'I heard you have got twenty-two stitches,' Mr Bensky said to Lola.

'We are so proud of you, darling,' said Mrs Bensky. 'Acute appendicitis and she didn't even complain!' Mrs Bensky added to a passing nurse.

Lola tried to listen to *Take It From Here* on the radio, but it hurt her too much when she laughed. The kids in Lola's class sent her a big box of chocolates, but she wasn't hungry.

Dr Stone smiled reassuringly as he took Lola's stitches out. 'Well, you're right as rain now. Don't carry anything too heavy for at least two weeks, and be careful going up and down stairs. You can go home tomorrow,' he said.

Lola went back to school on the first day that Dr Stone thought she was well enough.

In later years, Lola envied people who got bronchitis or chickenpox or ingrown toenails. Anything that wasn't really serious. Lola had trouble even catching a cold.

A Drive

She always called him 'Ma Motl'. They only had each other.
He called her 'Ma Nusia'. They were the same size. Both
short and round.

Nusia and Motl lived two doors from the Benskys. Every
summer, on the Australia Day weekend, the Benskys took
Nusia and Motl to Lorne for four days.

On the drives to Lorne, Nusia used to wear a pair of
underpants on her head. To protect her hair. Lola and Lina
had to stuff hankies in their mouths to stop their giggling.

Josl Bensky drove like a maniac. He had a need to
overtake everyone else on the road. Lola's job was to look
out for the police. She had to take this seriously, as it was
her fault each time he was booked for speeding.

Lola and Lina would glimpse the expressions on people's
faces as they caught the sight of Nusia with her pink silk
underpants flapping in the wind. The pain of the sisters'
suppressed laughter was agony.

Every now and then Renia Bensky would turn around
and glare at the girls. Before the trip she would tell the girls,
yet again, what good people Nusia and Motl were. 'Look,
so they don't have money. They've got big hearts, bigger
hearts than all the ones with big money. And they're poor
people, they haven't got children.'

This last poignant note never really rang true to the girls, as having children hadn't seemed to make their mother's life much happier.

All the Benskys' friends had come to this country fresh from Auschwitz or Dachau, or if they had been lucky, a couple of years buried in a bunker. But once here they had made it. They had nice houses, nice cars, big factories that were big business. They built flats that destroyed half of St Kilda and defaced the bayside beauty of Beaconsfield Parade.

Their kids weren't much good. Even Renia Bensky, although she tried to deny it, could see that. So what were Nusia and Motl missing?

Motl sat with his arm around Nusia, next to the girls in the back. They kept smiling. They were enjoying the trip, too. Nusia repeated the same stories of Lola's childhood. 'Remember, Motl, when she was a little girl? She would answer the phone: "Hello, this is little Lola. I'll talk to you."'

Josl, momentarily distracted from his goal of being first in line on the road, would launch into a diatribe about how nothing had changed, how much business he lost because no-one could get through to him on the phone at night. He would rant about the hours that Lola spent talking to girlfriends who, God help him, she'd only just left, after probably having talked to them at school all day. Renia, who didn't like most of Lola's friends, nodded in approval.

This distraction usually occurred on the Great Ocean Road, which curves and bends sharply alongside a drop of 500 feet to the sea. Every Christmas a car goes over the cliff.

Nusia and Motl smiled warmly. 'It's nice to be a good talker.' Nusia linked arms with Lola. The love flowed from her.

Nusia had the longest, most beautiful nails. They shone like dark red porcelain. Just as they arrived at the Lorne Hotel, Nusia would adjust the underpants with an elegant movement of the hands, smooth Motl's collar and sit back with an air of expectant excitement.

Every year the girls thought that she would take the underpants off before walking into the foyer. They prayed that she would take them off.

The front driveway of the hotel was full of people unpacking. They walked back and forth carrying fishing equipment, surfboards, rubber dinghies, beach mats, table-tennis bats, fly-spray and suntan lotions.

Lola and Lina looked at each other. It was one of their rare shared moments. Would she take them off? God, what if there were any boys watching? Could they stay in the car and find their rooms later? Would Renia miraculously understand and save them? How could they not hurt Motl's and Nusia's feelings?

Lina developed delayed car-sickness. Being sick worked miracles in the Bensky family; Lina was allowed to lie wanly on the back seat. Nusia looked at Lola. Through the ribboned pink lace frills, Lola could see the perfectly set blonde waves. 'Oy, Motl, such a sweet face she has. I baked such a lovely apple cake, no sugar, plenty of apples. Darling, carry it carefully.'

Lola carried the cake. Nusia and Motl walked either side of her.

'You know, darling,' Nusia said loudly, 'I've got a little piece of beautiful cheesecake in the bottom of the box. Mummy won't mind. It doesn't hurt to have one piece. Too thin doesn't look nice. Look at that one in her shorts. Looks like her mother doesn't feed her.'

Lola and Nusia and Motl stood in the queue checking in. Lola smoothed down her new gingham dress, held her stomach in and tried for her most sophisticated expression. Motl put his arm around Lola. 'Such a sweet girl.'

Nusia sighed in reply: 'Oy, Ma Motl, what a lovely holiday we're going to have.'

A Family Portrait

Renia Bensky's hair was slightly bouffant and stylishly cut short. Blonde, with coppery highlights glinting through – a colour that was very popular in Caulfield that year.

Laid out on the bed were a grey herringbone light wool tailored suit and a black and white spotted silk blouse with a once-again-fashionable Peter Pan collar. The sheer, fifteen-denier Smoky Nights pantihose screamed: 'High Leg. Sheer to the Waist.'

The herringbone suit sat smoothly on Renia. She patted her tummy with pleasure. It was always flat. Even when she sat down there was no bulge. All her friends admired her figure.

At the dinner parties she hosted every fifth Sunday night, Renia never sat down. All night she rushed between the dining room and the kitchen. Every fifth Sunday she served gefilte fish that everyone agreed was just right, not too sweet. Then came hot fried flounder in a sauce of onion, tomato and dill, followed by an entrée of chopped liver. The secret of Mrs Bensky's smoother, lighter chopped liver was simply an extra egg. One kilo of chicken livers, two large onions and five boiled eggs was the recipe she guarded with her life. The main course was a roast shoulder of veal with large, hot, boiled potatoes. If she could find a duck lean enough when she went shopping in Acland Street, she served roast duck.

The meal ended with Mrs Bensky's sponge cake. Mrs Bensky was famous all over Melbourne for her sponge cake. She told anyone who wanted to hear that her sponge cake was not fattening: it had only a tiny bit of sugar and hardly any flour. No-one was quite sure what held it together, but they ate it in large slices with relish, secure in the knowledge that it wasn't fattening.

Later in the evening, when the men settled down to play cards, usually gin rummy, and the women nestled in groups whispering, usually about their husbands and children, Mrs Bensky cleared the table, put out the chocolates and washed the dishes.

On the other Sunday nights, when it was Mrs Ganz's or Mrs Small's or Mrs Zelman's or Mrs Pekelman's turn to have dinner, Mrs Bensky helped. They could rely on her to serve the latkes straight from the frying pan, before the grated potato mixture became cold. Mrs Bensky would swiftly spoon out generous portions of cholent and kishke. Before anyone could say they were on a diet, their plates would be full of oxtail, baked for twenty-four hours in a glue of chicken fat, onions, garlic, lima beans, barley and potatoes.

Very few of the group had ever seen Mrs Bensky have a meal. For that matter, neither had her family. They had watched her chew a crust of toast while she prepared dinner, or have a bowl of semolina to soothe her nerves.

Six nights a week Mrs Bensky served grilled baby lamb chops with salad, grilled calf's liver with salad, grilled whiting with salad or a lean roast chicken with salad. The helpings always came in under five hundred calories. Mrs Bensky washed the dishes loudly while her family ate.

She often told her fat Lola how she herself had no tolerance for sweets. 'Do you ever see me with a chocolate? I can't eat them. They taste something terrible to me.' While she said this she glowed and looked even more beautiful.

Mr Bensky and the girls were quite self-sufficient. They didn't really need her meals. Mr Bensky kept a large supply of Toblerone bars in the glovebox of his new Fairlane. He did messages for Mrs Bensky willingly: some minced chicken from Rushinek's, some challah from Monarch's. Whenever she said 'Josl, can you pick up . . .?' he rose from his armchair. 'No trouble, Renia.' On the way he stopped at Leo's for a triple chocolate gelato.

Lola fed herself at Pellegrini's in Bourke Street on her way home from school, and Lina had a fast and accurate aim in and out of the fridge. She could remove a cheese blintz and digest it in ten seconds.

Mrs Bensky stepped into her shoes. Light grey suede, pointy-toed and soaring on six-inch stiletto heels, they were made by Maud Frizon of Paris and bought from Miss Louise of Collins Street, Melbourne. At Miss Louise's winter sale, Mrs Bensky paid £20 for these £79 shoes.

Mrs Bensky had a real eye for a bargain. She saved hundreds of pounds a week. Mrs Bensky personally knew every manufacturer of swimwear, evening wear, hosiery, overcoats, underwear, knitwear, furs, suits and sportswear within a ten-mile radius of Flinders Lane.

She walked briskly into the bathroom, relishing the feeling of power that came with the extra height. Searching in the lipstick drawer, she decided that Unspiced Rose by Estée Lauder was the right shade for today. First she outlined her lips with brown eyeliner pencil. Then she applied a thick, glossy coat of Unspiced Rose. Pleased with the result, she smiled at herself in the mirror.

The bathroom had sixty feet of mirror attached to sliding doors around three of its walls. These doors concealed endless shelves: shelves crammed with cleansers, toners, exfoliating creams, neck, chin and eye creams, thigh creams, day creams and night creams, clay and mud and apricot masks, ampoules for firming your skin and lifting

your breasts, cell extract treatments to remove wrinkles and dimples, and chimiozymolsat of yeast, which favourably affects the oxygen balance of epidermal tissue.

When Mr Bensky had built this oversized bathroom, he'd had high hopes of being able to shave in peace. Eventually, in despair, he'd removed his Remington electric razor with four different cutting blade selections and automatic overseas conversions to the small cupboard in the toilet next to the bathroom, and there he found his peace.

Mr Bensky spent two hours a day in the toilet, between 7 a.m. and 8 a.m., and again from 9 p.m. to 10 p.m. The seemingly endless stream of volcanic farts erupting from him in there was a source of excruciating embarrassment for Lola, whose bedroom was across the hallway. If she had a girlfriend staying overnight, Lola set the alarm clock for six-thirty. At five to seven she nonchalantly turned her transistor on to full volume. Johnny O'Keefe screaming 'Shout' at the top of his lungs on 3UZ was barely a match for Mr Bensky's early-morning evacuation.

Touching up her eyelashes, already lengthened and strengthened by Fabulash, Mrs Bensky reminded herself that it was their turn to pay for the pictures this Saturday. She looked up the phone number of the Rivoli and rang straight away, because it wasn't always easy to get seventeen seats on a Saturday night.

The gang, as Lola called them – the Benskys, the Smalls, the Ganzes, the Zelmans and the Pekelmans – were joined by the Feiglins, the Glicks, the Blatmans and poor divorced Mr Berman for their regular Saturday-night excursion to the pictures.

They'd seen almost every film shown in Melbourne since 1952. Mrs Bensky thought of herself as the intellectual of the group. She liked *Wild Strawberries* and *Last Year at Marienbad*, while others enjoyed *The Pink Panther* and *My Fair Lady*.

At interval, Mr Bensky liked to be the one to buy the snacks. He could get as much as he needed, and it was dizzyingly satisfying for him to buy scorched almonds for seventeen people. Seventeen people could eat a lot of scorched almonds. Mr Bensky liked to make sure that nobody missed out.

Sometimes after the film they went to a supper dance at the Top Hat cabaret. Mr Ganz, with his lean figure and cornflower-blue eyes, was unanimously recognized as the most handsome man in the group. He danced with Mrs Bensky. The knowledge that they made a stunning couple swept them through the quickstep with even greater grace.

Mrs Zelman danced with Mr Bensky, who could be relied upon to have a few leftover scorched almonds in his jacket pocket. They ate them with a furtive happiness while they foxtrotted in the far corner of the dance floor. Mrs Ganz and Mr Zelman often danced the cha-cha and the rumba together. They both liked the livelier dances.

Mrs Glick and Mrs Small and Mrs Blatman and Mrs Feiglin and Mrs Bensky took it in turns to dance with Mr Berman. In the last few years Mr Berman had become even more nervous and distant. He hadn't gone out with a woman since his disastrous affair with Mrs McKenzie ended in 1962.

Their affair had thrown the entire group into turmoil. The group had all made sure their children had grown up understanding that it was essential to have a Jewish partner. Now, here was one of their close friends infatuated with a shikse, holding her hand in Carlisle Street and grinning like a fifteen-year-old. Mrs Glick and Mrs Feiglin decided that she was after his money. They visited Mrs McKenzie privately. They offered her five hundred pounds to stop seeing Mr Berman. Mrs McKenzie offered the women tea and biscuits. Ten days later she was gone. She had moved to Moe to be closer to her mother, a broken Mr Berman told the group.

The phone rang. Mrs Bensky, who was just about to put the final coat of Imbi's Mellow Mauve on her nails, shook her head in annoyance. It was probably Mr Bensky calling from Myers to say that there was no white Tissus Michel material left. She should have bought it when she saw it there last week, she admonished herself. She knew she looked good in white, and could wear it without any worry about its fattening effect.

She answered the phone. It was Mrs Ganz. Mrs Bensky cradled the phone on her shoulder with her upper arm. She swung her nails to and fro to catch the dry breeze of the air-conditioning. 'Renia darling, I don't think we will go to the pictures tomorrow, darling. Moishe has a terrible cold. I asked him to go to the doctor because I'm sure he has got a virus, but you know Moishe, stubborn like an ox. Me, myself, I've got a sore throat already. So, Renia darling, make it fifteen tickets.'

Mrs Bensky nurtured a not-so-secret dislike of Mrs Ganz. Mrs Bensky knew that Mrs Ganz thought of herself as highly intelligent and very beautiful. Mrs Bensky reassured herself that anyone could see that Mrs Ganz was no beauty. The fact that the Ganzes' Champs Elysees Blouses had one hundred and seventy-eight retail outlets around Australia did not mean that Mrs Ganz was intelligent. Mrs Bensky bit her lip, thinking about the many very stupid people she knew who were good at business.

Mrs Bensky toasted herself a slice of black rye bread. It was so black it could have passed for pumpernickel. Mrs Bensky liked peace and quiet when she ate. She was comforted by the warm density of the thick toast.

When Mr and Mrs Bensky arrived in Australia, Mr Bensky had wanted to abbreviate their name to Benn, but Mrs Bensky liked the name Bensky. She didn't want to change it. Many people had changed their names when they came to Australia. The Silberbergs, the Rotkleins, the Mokruschkis, the Pirkoskis and the Minofskis had become the

Silvers, the Rotes, the Moors, the Pikes and the Mints. They now sounded like a gathering of good Presbyterians.

As Renia Kindler of Lodz, and then Renia Bensky, Mrs Bensky had been the most beautiful girl in the town, some said in the whole of Poland. Her red-brown hair was waist-length and flowed behind her like a dark curtain, framing her high pink cheekbones and intense eyes. Even though she was from one of the poorer families in Lodz, with no dowry to speak of, she was constantly pursued by admirers.

She was also very clever. In later years Mrs Bensky never tired of telling her two daughters: 'I gave maths tuitions', which she always pronounced 'choosons', 'to pay for my schooling, from when I was eight. I was always very good at mathematics. I was the only Jewish girl to finish high school in Lodz and be offered a place at university.'

As Mrs Bensky was about to begin her first year of medicine at the University of Vienna, the war broke out. Six years later Mrs Bensky graduated from Auschwitz.

Mr Bensky was a good husband. He had always been grateful to Mrs Bensky for marrying him. His family were displeased by the marriage, for they were property owners and timber merchants, and one of the wealthiest Jewish families in Lodz. Mr Bensky still felt upset when he remembered the hysteria he'd caused in his family when he had married Mrs Bensky. All that fuss and all that heart-ache, and all for nothing, because soon they were all in concentration camp and equally poor.

To give Mrs Bensky a break, Mr Bensky took Lina and Lola out on Saturday afternoons. When the girls were smaller they would go to the zoo. Mr Bensky enjoyed those afternoons. He would sit in the small park next to the bandstand and read the latest Perry Mason thriller. Lina and Lola would wave to him from the top of the elephant, which walked round and round the track circling the park. Lina and Lola liked to buy ten tickets each. That way they stayed on the elephant for exactly an hour. This suited Mr

Bensky. When the hour was up, the three of them walked to the kiosk and bought six Eskimo Pies. Then they strolled around, looking at the animals. When she was older, Lola looked back on those afternoons as the nicest part of her childhood.

If there was a new show on at the Tivoli, Mr Bensky took the girls there on Saturday afternoons. They saw acts from all over the world. Sexy dancers and all sorts of singers, acrobats and jugglers, exotic striptease artists, a blonde underwater stripper, comedians and performing dogs, magicians and evil-looking hypnotists.

Hundreds of semi-nude, beautiful showgirls decorated the stage. The showgirls wore high heels and high-cut fishnet tights. On their heads they balanced spectacular soaring head-dresses made from hundreds of brightly coloured feathers and sequins. By law the showgirls had to stand perfectly still. They were not allowed to move at all. From their front-row seats, Mr Bensky and the girls had a very good view.

The comedians were Mr Bensky's favourites. He laughed at their jokes so heartily that other people in the theatre stood up to see who was laughing like that. Sometimes he laughed so hard that his shirt buttons popped and tears ran down his face. Sometimes Lola worried that he would burst with happiness. At interval they always shared a packet of Jaffas, a packet of Fantales and a packet of Columbines.

Mr Bensky applauded each act vigorously and was the first to leap onto the stage if a juggler, hypnotist, comedian or magician asked for volunteers from the audience.

Now, Mrs Bensky was starting to feel edgy. A faint headache hovered at the back of her head. Mr Bensky should have been home by now. She'd told him that the photographer was due at two o'clock.

She parted the plush gold velvet curtains in the family room. Outside it was sunny. Mrs Bensky was pleased. Later on she could lie out on the grass for half an hour or so.

Mrs Bensky had a deep golden tan all year round. She saw her suntan as public evidence of her energy, vitality and youthful spirit.

When Mrs Bensky lay in the sun, she could think about her daughters without anxiety. In the sun she could forget about Lola's weight and not worry about whether Lina would ever find a boyfriend. Sometimes a ray of pleasure crept through Mrs Bensky's thoughts about her daughters; at least neither of her children had ever had an abortion or experimented with drugs.

Mrs Bensky liked to sunbathe in solitude. At home this was easy, for Mr Bensky loathed the sun. Even on his summer holidays he spent his time indoors reading Raymond Chandler. Lina had very pale skin, which blistered if she crossed Collins Street in the sun, and Lola was too embarrassed to put her flesh, olive though it was, into a bathing suit.

There was a loud knock at the front door. 'Renia, Renia darling, it's Josl.' Mrs Bensky switched off the indoor and outdoor burglar alarms and Mr Bensky unlocked the mortice lock and Lockwood deadlock. He was beaming. 'Darling, I went to Buckleys and I went to Georges and I had no luck. And then I had a very good idea, I went to Yanek at the top of Bourke Street and Yanek had two and a half yards of white Tissus Michel.'

Mrs Bensky looked at him. 'Josl, you know I need three yards for a dress.' Mr Bensky lost his beam.

Mrs Bensky had prepared Mr Bensky's lunch: four slices of Pariser sausage, a tomato quartered, two radishes, a spring onion, some lettuce and three Vita-Wheat biscuits. On their bed she had laid out Mr Bensky's new white shirt, a finely striped maroon and gold tie, and Mr Bensky's best suit, which was grey with cream flecks. Mr Bensky ate and got dressed.

At exactly two o'clock Michael Beets, the most successful

and talented Jewish photographer in Melbourne, arrived with his assistant.

Every year Michael Beets photographed the Bensky family. Mrs Bensky chose the photograph she liked best and ordered a twenty-by-thirty-inch copy, which she put into an ornate gilt-edged frame and displayed with great pride in the lounge room.

'Good afternoon, Mrs Bensky. You look wonderful. You're getting younger every day. It's true, you look more beautiful every year. It's a pleasure to see you.'

'Oh, Mr Beets, I look terrible. I've got a headache and I've had sinus trouble for three weeks. I've taken Amoxil and Abbocillin and Moxacin and nothing helps. Look at how my nose is swollen.'

Lina and Lola arrived separately, at the same time. Mr Bensky kissed Lina hello. Lina had a habit of averting her head when she was kissed, so that the kisser came in contact with a mouthful of hair and the back of her head.

Lola picked up the book that Lina had bought her parents as a gift. It was inscribed: 'To the best Mum and Dad in the world.' Lola felt nauseous with disgust.

'Lola darling,' her mother was saying. Lola looked up, still feeling sick. 'Maybe you'd like to put on a little bit of mascara?' Mrs Bensky trilled.

'No thanks, Mum.' Lola walked away, smoothing down her dress, which had bat-wing sleeves, was gathered at the yoke and was made out of satiny, black crushed velvet. The dress flowed past Lola's hips, the part of Lola that Lola tried to hide, against all odds.

'OK, OK, OK, everybody,' Mr Beets called as he shepherded them into the dining room. The dining room was low-ceilinged and rectangular. The bottom panels of the windows, which overlooked the garden, were made of opaque blue glass, a style that was fashionable in Caulfield and East St Kilda in the 1960s. Lola called it Jewish-Chinese architecture.

The Bensky family stood in a row. Mr Bensky patted a block of Small's Energy chocolate in his pocket. Lina blinked rapidly, her face twisted with tension. Lola arranged herself so that she stood between but slightly behind Mr and Mrs Bensky, a position that she hoped would cut her hips down a bit. Mrs Bensky glowed. Her eyes were luminous. A soft expression of serenity lit her face. Everything was ready. One, two, three, click. They smiled for the camera.

What Do You Know About Friends?

In Renia Bensky's world, people were pigs. 'Don't be a greedy pig,' she would say when Lola reached for another potato. Renia's neighbour, Mrs Spratt, was 'a dirty pig'. Her favourite grandchild was 'a little piggy', her cousin Adek 'a big pig'.

Josl chauffeured his two daughters around every Saturday morning. To the city, to the dressmaker, to the hairdresser. On the way home he liked to stop and buy himself a double chocolate gelato. 'What a pig!' Renia said when they arrived home.

When Renia talked about Josl's father, who had died in the ghetto, she said, 'such a pig'. Sometimes she would say a bit more, although the past, their lives before they came to Australia, was definitely out of bounds, their own private territory. Sometimes a small sliver of detail would slip out. 'Such a pig he was. In the ghetto he cried because he was so hungry. Children were dead in the streets and he was crying because he was hungry.'

Until she was twenty Lola had never seen a pig. When she saw her first pigs, she was fascinated by how unselfconscious they were. They snorted their way through their food, big and pink and bulky. They weren't holding their stomachs flat or sucking in their cheeks. They weren't expecting judgements. They seemed quite happy to be pigs.

If people weren't pigs, then they were idiots. Even when she was quite small Lola knew that Mrs Bensky was an authority on pigs and idiots. 'Such an idiot!' Mrs Bensky would shout. 'Such an idiot is that Mrs Berman. An idiot, an i-d-i-o-t. She thinks she speaks a perfect English. In the butcher I heard her say "Cut me in half please." Such a perfect English!'

Mrs Berman had been Mrs Bensky's friend. Until Mrs Berman left Mr Berman and Mrs Bensky could no longer be friends with her, the two women had baked cakes in Mrs Bensky's kitchen on Saturday afternoons. Mrs Berman made her honeycake and rugelachs and Mrs Bensky baked her lakech. Working in the kitchen together, they looked like good friends.

'Friends,' Mrs Bensky said to Lola. 'What do you know about friends? Friends, pheh! You can trust only your family.'

And what did Lola know? She had watched the Benskys and their friends, their 'company', as they called themselves. The company went to the pictures together every Saturday night and then to supper afterwards. On Sunday evenings they played cards. If there was a good show on, sometimes they went out during the week. They celebrated each other's birthdays, anniversaries, barmitzvahs, engagements and weddings, and were present at the operations, illnesses and funerals.

Lola thought that the company were family. She called them Uncle and Aunty and believed that they would always care about her. What did Lola know?

Mrs Bensky hated Mrs Ganz. She was irritated by the way that Mrs Ganz kept inviting her to fashion parades, card afternoons and charity luncheons. Couldn't Mrs Ganz see that she was very busy? Every day Mrs Bensky had to wash six sheets, four pillow cases, three eiderdown covers and seven towels. She had to scrub and polish the floors, and vacuum the carpets. And on top of this she had to cook and to wash up. She was not the kind of woman who had time to go to a fashion parade. Why couldn't Mrs Ganz understand this?

Mrs Bensky thought that Mrs Ganz had always been spoilt. In the ghetto Mrs Ganz's father had been a Jewish 'policeman'. Their family had rarely been hungry. In 1943 they were smuggled out of the ghetto and spent the rest of the war hiding in a cellar. Mrs Bensky often chatted to Mrs Pekelman on the phone. She felt that Genia Pekelman had her problems, but above all she had a good heart. Mrs Bensky advised Mrs Pekelman about which clothes suited her best, how to cook a good gulah, where to buy the freshest Murray Perch. She also shared some beauty tips with her, including the fact that if you rinsed your hair with a bit of beer after washing it the waves stayed in much longer. Renia Bensky and Genia Pekelman, both non-drinkers, often trailed an alcoholic air around with them.

Lola learnt about friendship from listening to the two women on the phone. Last week Mrs Bensky had said in an affectionate tone, 'Genia darling, I bumped into Yetta Kauffman in the city. Such an ugly face that woman has got. You think you are ugly, Genia darling? Next to Yetta Kauffman you are a big beauty.'

This may have seemed harsh to an outsider, but Lola knew that it was affectionate and well-intentioned. In this company one of the friendliest and most enthusiastic responses to anything was: 'What, what, you are crazy or something?'

Things cooled off between Renia Bensky and Genia Pekelman when Genia took up dancing lessons. She was forty-seven. At thirteen, Genia had been a promising young dancer. She had won a ballet scholarship to study in Paris. She was counting the days to her fourteenth birthday, waiting to leave for Paris, when the Germans arrived in Warsaw.

Now, Mrs Pekelman was learning Indian dance. She went to dancing classes twice a week. She was taught by

Madame Sanrit. Mrs Pekelman wore leotards under her sari and practised at home every afternoon. She loved to dance and danced at every opportunity.

If a group of women were having a charity luncheon, Mrs Pekelman asked if she could dance at the lunch. When Mrs Pekelman learnt that Mrs Small was taking a group of voluntary Jewish Welfare kitchen helpers on a tour of the Victorian National Gallery, she begged her to bring the group to her home, where she would dance for them.

Some of the company were embarrassed by Genia Pekelman and her dancing. Mrs Small was furious. She said to Mrs Bensky, 'Look at her! She is so big and fat and ugly, and she wants to dance for everybody. When she moves her big tuches around the room it is shocking.'

'She can't help it,' Mrs Bensky replied. 'She doesn't know how she looks. She is not so intelligent.'

As well as pigs and idiots, Mrs Bensky knew about intelligence. She dismissed most people as 'not intelligent'. One year Mrs Small, who spoke Russian, Polish, Yiddish, French and English, interpreted for the members of the Moscow Circus when they came to Melbourne. Mrs Bensky was clenched with anger for the entire season.

'She thinks she is such a big intelligence,' Mrs Bensky railed. 'What does she read, this big intelligence, this Mrs Intelligentsia? Maybe a *Women's Weekly* under the hair dryer once a week? I remember her mother delivered our milk in Lodz. Two big cans across her shoulders, she walked from house to house in bare feet. And both daughters finished school at twelve. Now, suddenly, Ada Small is a genius. She tells everybody that she matriculated in Poland. Soon she will say she was almost a doctor. Everybody who came here after the war was almost a doctor. Mrs Ada Intelligentsia thinks she is important because she is translating for an acrobat.'

Mrs Bensky did know about intelligence. She was the only one of the group who had been at university. She still kept her student card in her handbag. In 1972, Mrs Bensky enrolled at Melbourne University. She did one semester of 'Physics In The Firing Line'. Lola had suggested that Mrs Bensky study Russian or German, languages she was fluent in. Lola thought that this would have been a gentler introduction to university life, but Mrs Bensky insisted on 'Physics In The Firing Line'. Science had been Mrs Bensky's great love in Lodz. When she spoke about Copernicus and the planets, Mrs Bensky was at her most tender. It was science that Mrs Bensky wanted to go back to.

In Lodz, Mrs Bensky came top of her class every year. She was every teacher's favourite student. Her curiosity was as immense as her ambition. Other people in the neighbourhood laughed at her father for wasting his money on a daughter. 'You'll make her too clever for a husband,' one neighbour repeated regularly.

At the University of Melbourne, Renia Bensky was so tense she could hardly hear the lecturer. His words flew around the auditorium. Mrs Bensky had to grab each word and put it in its correct place. Sometimes she lost a few words and the sentences didn't make sense. She sat in a sweat through most of the professor's speeches. Later she learnt that this heat was menopausal.

Renia worked feverishly on her first assignment, 'Molecules and The Future'. At last it was finished. Fifteen pages on bright yellow notepaper. Lina corrected the English, and they hired a professional typist to type the essay.

Mrs Bensky got a 'C' for 'Molecules and The Future'. She wept and wept.

Mr Bensky tried to comfort her. 'This assignment, Renia darling, is out of this world. Something special. There is no question about it. It is perfect, believe me.' But Mrs Bensky went on weeping.

Mrs Small gave Mrs Bensky her sympathy and support. 'I think it is anti-Semitism,' she said. 'For what other reason would he give such a beautiful piece of work only a "C"? He is an anti-Semite, for sure.'

Most of the company called around to offer their condolences. They knew it wasn't Mrs Bensky's fault. A 'C'
for Renia Bensky, whoever heard of such a thing? Everybody knew she was too intelligent. But Mrs Bensky was
inconsolable.

She rang her tutor, a young, pale-faced boy of twenty-
five, to ask if maybe it was her English that wasn't perfect.
Maybe that was why she had got a 'C'.

'Excuse me, tutor,' she began, 'I want to know if you
have made a mistake with my essay. I think the English was
very good. My younger daughter who is a lawyer with an
honours degree did correct my writing, so it couldn't be my
bad English. And my English is very good. She didn't find
many mistakes at all. I understand you did give young John
Matheson an "A". Well, he told me himself that I did
understand the molecules much better than him. In fact, I
explained some of the facts to him. So, he got an "A" and I
got a "C"? Maybe I shouldn't have hired a typist? Maybe
you think I have got money to burn or to throw away that I
hired a typist? My husband worked very hard for fifteen
years in factories so I could afford a typist. Maybe you were
prejudiced against my typing? Did Mr Matheson type his
essay? I'm sure not. As a matter of fact I know his mother,
Mrs Matheson. She told me he was talking about how much
I know about molecules. You know, I, myself, don't think
you are an anti-Semite. My friend Mrs Small does, but she
is not intelligent. She doesn't see we are in a modern world
and this is not Poland.

'So, do you have an answer, Mr Tutor? Do you know
how many years I dreamed of going to university? Do you
know this? I dreamed of studying at university when I was a
small girl. And I kept dreaming. Even in Auschwitz, when
I didn't dream any more, sometimes when I was standing in
roll-call for six hours, barefoot in the snow, I would try to
think about what subjects I could study one day.'

Now Mrs Bensky was crying. 'Do you have an answer,
Mr Tutor? When I came to Australia my sister-in-law said

to me that all women work in Australia. She said to me I should have considered if I could afford to have a baby before I got pregnant. So I took my baby every day to Mrs Polonsky, a woman in Carlton. I had never been apart from my baby. Sometimes I vomited on the tram on the way to the factory. I felt so frightened. Josl told me that Mrs Polonsky was a good woman and nothing would happen to little Lola, but I couldn't stop being frightened. When I finished work I picked Lolala up. Mrs Polonsky lived just next to the university, and when I stopped vomiting, I made myself a promise that one day I would go there. Did you hear me, Mr Tutor?'

Mrs Bensky left 'Physics In The Firing Line' six weeks after she had begun. She left the University of Melbourne a wiser person. The rest of the company acknowledged this and accorded her new respect. 'She studied at Melbourne University,' they now said when they spoke of her.

I Wonder Why She Looks So Happy

Genia Pekelman looked at herself in the mirror. Her thighs looked strong. They were muscular, not fat. Her breasts had fallen, but they were looking better than they used to. Less limp.

She positioned herself in front of the full-length mirror, adjusted the legs of her leotards and began to dance.

Genia felt alive. She could feel her muscles. She could feel her heart. She could feel her strength.

She moved gracefully and rhythmically. She moved in time to the chorus of her veins and arteries. In tune with the movement of her blood.

Her head and arms and legs were in harmony with the stars and the moon and the sun. That was how Genia Pekelman felt. Connected. Anchored. Part of the world.

When Genia Pekelman was dancing, she could forget everything else. Genia had a lot to forget. She often thought that she had so much to forget that she could dance her way through ten lifetimes and still not have danced enough to forget everything.

The memories that Genia Pekelman was trying to forget would leap out unexpectedly and leave her breathless.

Last week, in Pruzansky's butcher shop, a customer had asked for a kilo of calf's liver. Mr Pruzansky was carefully slicing the liver. His blade was sharp and slid easily through

the soft liver. Genia was watching, but she saw another
blade slicing another liver.

She saw Shimek Greenbaum cutting a liver with a blunt
piece of tin. The liver belonged to Abe Korner. This was in
Bergen-Belsen, in the last few weeks before the camp was
liberated. Genia had just turned nineteen. Germany was
losing the war. The front lines were disintegrating. The
Germans were evacuating their forced-labour camps and
concentration camps. Thousands of prisoners were brought
to Bergen-Belsen on foot and by rail. In the week of Genia's
nineteenth birthday, in April 1945, twenty-eight thousand
new inmates were dumped into Bergen-Belsen.

Typhoid raged. Corpses rotted in the barracks. Rats ate
prisoners' fingers and toes while they slept. And starving
prisoners ate the inmates who had died.

There were things that Genia kept forgetting, memories
that she fought to remember. Genia struggled to retain a
clear picture of her parents.

Shmul and Mania Buchbinder, Genia's parents, were
both dentists. Genia was their only child. They doted on
her. Genia had piano lessons and ballet classes. A tutor
came to the house twice a week to teach Genia French. At
ten, Genia had read *Madame Bovary* in French.

Mania and Shmul had such hopes for their beautiful and
clever Genia. Mania would tell Genia about the writers and
the musicians they had had in the family. For hundreds of
years the Buchbinders had produced extraordinarily gifted
people.

Shmul's mother, Yetta, was one of the best-loved Yiddish actresses in Poland. Genia adored her grandmother,
and often travelled with her parents from their home in
Lowicz to watch Yetta Buchbinder perform in Warsaw.
'What fine silk you are spun from, my child,' Genia's
mother used to say to her.

Genia was pampered by all of her relatives in Lowicz.
Her uncles brought her presents from Europe, and her
aunties combed and plaited her long auburn hair. Genia

never minded being an only child. She felt as though she had many mothers and fathers and many brothers and sisters.

Mania and Shmul Buchbinder died in Auschwitz. Yetta Buchbinder died in the Warsaw ghetto. All the aunties and uncles died. There had been eighty-seven Buchbinders in Lowicz. After the war, Genia was the only one left.

At home this morning, Genia was practising her arabesques. For a few years she had studied Indian dance. She had enjoyed that, but it was ballet that made Genia Pekelman truly happy.

Genia was in the Advanced Senior class at the Dancing Academy in Brighton. She was the oldest member of the class. She was twice as old as her teacher.

Genia knew that people laughed at her. Sometimes she laughed at herself too. Sometimes she could see that she looked absurd. A crazy woman. There she was, fifty years old, the owner of eight pairs of leotards, endless leg-warmers, and two white tutus!

Genia didn't mind people laughing. They were not her real audience. When Genia danced she was in another world. She wasn't in Melbourne. She wasn't in Bergen-Belsen. She was in a dream. This dream was in a place where everything was as it would have been if it were not for the war.

Her parents were there. Her grandmother was there. Her uncles and aunties were there. They had all known that Genia would be a ballerina, and they were such an appreciative audience. This morning Yetta had clapped and clapped when Genia had balanced an arabesque perfectly. Her ballet teacher from Lowicz, Madame Kasner, was there. Last week Madame Kasner had said to Genia, 'Genia darling, we have to be grateful to Olga Ramanova, who told us when you were six that you would be a great dancer. Do you remember when she performed in Lowicz?'

Of course Genia remembered Olga Ramanova. The Rus-

sian ballerina had patted Genia on the head, and told her that if she practised hard she could possibly one day dance with the greatest of the Russian ballet companies. And little Genia had practised and practised.

Last Thursday Genia had danced for a small group. It was the Eastern Division Bridge Players' luncheon. Genia knew that some of the women were mocking her, and that the rest of them felt sorry for her. After her performance, Genia was getting dressed in the bathroom when she heard Mina Blatt say to Marilla Rose: 'It looks something shocking to see a woman of her age jumping around as if she is a young girl. I wonder why she looks so happy.'

'You are right, Mina,' said Marilla. 'Who knows why she looks so happy?'

Genia had been dancing for forty-five minutes when the telephone rang. It was Renia Bensky. Renia had rung to see if Genia needed any towels. Josl was going in to Shavinsky's warehouse. Both women had linen cupboards large enough to service a small hospital.

'All right, Renia, ask Josl to buy me six of those nice cream bath-size towels.'

Genia could never have too many sheets or towels. The feeling of clean, pure cotton sheets on her bed gave her such a sense of well-being. It was the same with good towels. Genia felt pampered and indulged every morning when she dried herself with the thick, king-sized bath towels.

'I'll bring you the towels on Saturday,' said Renia. 'I can't speak to you for too long today, because I have to cook something for Lola. I am cooking her a cabbage and rice dish. It is her new diet. I make a big pot for the whole week. But, Genia, I looked at Lola last week, and to tell you the truth, I think she is eating the whole pot in one night. Then she goes on another diet for the other days. I don't know what to do. It's killing me.'

Genia felt depressed about Lola. Lola had been a beautiful little girl. With her dark, sausage curls and her lively

eyes, she had looked like a doll. Now she was very fat, and
her eyes were flat.

'Renia,' Genia said, 'shall we go together to the German
Embassy? I have to go this week. Why don't we go together
again?'

Renia and Genia received 'reparation' money from the
German government. Genia got slightly more than Renia
because she had been a teenager during the war. The
German government, Genia's lawyer had told her, considered it had more to make up for to those people who had
also lost their youth.

Renia had been eligible for this extra payment, as she had
only been twenty-one when she arrived in Auschwitz, but
by the time Renia found out about the extra 'reparation'
money the German government's deadline for applications
had passed.

The amount of money that they received was such a
pittance that to label it 'reparation' and 'restitution' was
offensive. Some Jews refused to accept this money, but to
most Jews it was an important symbolic gesture.

The 'reparation' money, Josl was fond of saying, was not
enough to cover the monthly ice-cream bills he used to run
up in Lodz.

Once a year, all the Jews receiving these payments had to
present themselves to the German Embassy, to prove that
they were still alive.

Last year Renia and Genia had gone to the German
Embassy together. Genia had picked Renia up and the two
women, who talked on the telephone for an hour every day,
had driven to South Yarra in silence.

'Well, can you see that I am alive?' Renia had asked the
man at the German Embassy.

'Yes, Madam, I can see that,' he had said.

'Well, you are blind, sir,' Renia had said. 'Because you
killed all of us. Those of us who are still walking and talking
are not alive, sir.'

Afterwards the two women had walked along Punt Road

to the car. A sudden feeling of lightness had come over Genia. She was alive, and she wanted to prove it. 'Renia,' she had said, 'let's go shopping and spend this "reparation" money all at once. Let's decide what we can do with it. Should we invest it in BHP, Renia, or should we buy a pair of shoes?'

Renia and Genia had driven into the city. They had gone to Miss Louise in Collins Street and bought a pair of Maud Frizon shoes each.

'All right, Genia,' Renia said. 'We will go to the embassy together again. Is Tuesday morning all right for you?'

'I'll pick you up at ten o'clock, after my ballet class,' said Genia.

'Genia darling,' said Renia. 'I have been thinking about Pola Ganz and Joseph Zelman. I think that there is something funny going on between them. It would be shocking. After all, Moishe is a wonderful husband to Pola. What is that crazy woman doing? At her age she needs to shtoop so much? And what about poor Mina Zelman? I know that she is very tall, and maybe Joseph needs to feel he is a big man, so he shtoops with little Pola Ganz. But there are other ways of being a big man. What's happening to the world today, Genia? I remember when I thought that we had had so much pain and suffering that we would never cause pain or suffering to each other. I was stupid.'

It worried Genia that Renia was so suspicious. If Pola and Joseph were having an affair, then it had probably been going on for a long time and not hurting anybody. Who knows whether they are or they are not? thought Genia. She didn't care.

What had gone wrong with Renia Bensky? Genia wondered. When Genia had first met Renia in 1950, Renia had been so kind. Renia was still hopeful then. Later she had hardened. They had probably all hardened, thought Genia.

What had been taken away from them in the war, Genia thought, what they had lost, was their trust. Renia had never regained her trust. She was suspicious of everything. In 1950, thought Genia, Renia had still thought that she would be able to regain her trust.

'Anyway, I am not going to think about Joseph Zelman and dear Pola Ganz any more. I have got better things to worry about,' said Renia. 'Poor Lina, she has got this week such an allergy. It wasn't enough that she did become allergic to food, now she is allergic to her dog. And she loves her Pandy so much. Such a stupid dog, and she loves him.'

Renia had talked for months about Lina's allergy to food. 'Poor Lina,' she had said to anyone who would listen, and many who didn't want to hear. 'She eats nothing at all. As soon as she puts anything into her mouth, she puts on half a stone. So, she eats nothing. The doctors said it was an allergy to food. My poor Lina is allergic to food.'

Genia's husband, Izak, was sceptical. 'She doesn't eat anything and she puts on weight? It doesn't sound like an allergy to me. Maybe Lina could market this allergy. If the doctors could find out how a person can eat nothing and not die, we can save the whole Third World.'

After talking for fifteen minutes about Lina's blotches caused by her allergy to her dog, Renia was sounding a bit flat. 'How is Esther?' she said.

Esther Pekelman, Genia's younger daughter, stammered. She couldn't finish her sentences. Esther's thoughts always trailed off in a nervous stutter. All the fears that Genia managed to contain, Esther displayed. In many ways Esther was a barometer for the whole Pekelman family. If things were difficult for the family, Esther wore the symptoms of that distress. When times were calmer, Esther looked better.

Genia felt closer to Esther than she did to Rachel, her first-born daughter. Genia felt that Esther understood her. Esther had been in the audience at the luncheon last week. As soon as the performance was over, Esther had rushed up to her. 'You were fabulous, Mum,' she had said. She had hugged Genia tightly. It had been a hug that had shut out all Genia's fears and nerves. Esther didn't have the beauty of her sister, Rachel, but Esther had the heart.

Genia thought that Rachel was one of the most beautiful young women she had ever seen. Many other people thought the same thing about Rachel. Rachel had large, green, almond-shaped eyes, flawless olive skin and an elegant aquiline nose. Her face was framed by a head of thick auburn ringlets. At the moment Rachel was between husbands. She had divorced number three, and had just met Boris Zayer, who fulfilled all the prerequisites for husband number four.

Each of Rachel's husbands had been richer than the husband before him. Rachel had started by marrying a struggling young lawyer. She had left that marriage with a small house in South Yarra. Rachel's last divorce had netted her a settlement of two and a half million dollars.

'She doesn't have an economics degree or a Diploma of Business Administration, but she could be president of the World Bank, the way that she has escalated her assets so rapidly,' Izak used to say about his elder daughter.

Rachel was now beautiful and rich. She believed that every man in Melbourne was in love with her. She had told Genia that Rabbi Blatt had propositioned her at her son's barmitzvah. She had also said that the rabbi who had handled her last divorce had wanted to handle her. Genia couldn't believe that a rabbi would behave like that. 'Rachel darling,' she had said to her daughter, 'I think you must have made a mistake. Rabbis are more concerned with the Torah than a nice-looking tuches.'

With her striking curls and smooth skin and polished nails, Rachel looked full of life, but Genia knew that there was not a lot of joy in Rachel. Rachel was made happy by the transient things in life, and she had to keep getting more and more of them. Esther, Rachel thought, had more life-force in her, more spirituality, more balance. Yet to most people, Genia thought, Rachel appeared alive, and Esther appeared mad.

'Esther is fine,' Genia said to Renia.

'It's lucky that she's got a good husband like Stan,' said Renia. 'Someone like Esther is not always appreciated. What do people appreciate?' continued Renia. 'They appreciate the things that are not so important. Do you remember what Rabbi Bloom said when he married Stan and Esther? He said Esther had a good heart. Usually Rabbi Bloom says that the bride is beautiful. If he can't say that she is beautiful, he says she is clever. If he can't say clever or beautiful, he says how rich the parents are. He doesn't say rich, he says successful, but everyone understands what he is saying. And if he can't say one of those things, Rabbi Bloom says that the bride has got a good heart. When Rabbi Bloom said Esther had a good heart, I did nearly cry, Genia.'

Genia thought that this was a good time to say goodbye to Renia. She could feel herself starting to feel gloomy.

'Genia darling, before you hang up,' said Renia, 'please let me make an appointment to the hairdressers for you. Ada Small rang me this morning to say that she heard Malka Spiel and Fela Brot in the chicken shop saying that it was shocking that a woman of your age has such long hair. Genia, I am telling you this for your own good. Do you want people to talk more about you?'

Genia had been growing her hair for four years. It had almost reached her waist. She wore it in a single plait.

'Don't listen to them,' Izak had said when Genia had told him about Renia and Ada nagging her to have her hair cut. 'If it makes you happy to have long hair, then have long hair,' Izak had said.

'Renia darling,' said Genia, 'I know that you tell me these things for my own good, but it is me that people are talking about, and I don't mind. At least I am giving people

something to talk about. I have to go now, Renia. I will
speak to you tomorrow. Goodbye.'

Genia felt unsettled now. She should take the phone off the
hook when she wanted to practise her ballet. She had tried
to take the phone off the hook many times, but she was
always overcome with the worry that Izak or Rachel or
Esther might want to get through to her and not be able to.

She really had to make sure that she could practise
uninterrupted, Genia thought. She would never progress if
her practice was constantly interrupted. She would take the
phone off the hook. She would do it today, Genia decided.
She took the phone off the hook, and walked back to
Rachel's old bedroom, which was now Genia's rehearsal
room.

Last night Josl Bensky had gently asked Genia why she
drove herself so hard to dance. 'I feel happy when I am
dancing,' she had replied. 'When I'm dancing, Josl, I feel
very happy, and it takes my mind off things.'

Josl understood about taking your mind off things. Josl
read three or four detective novels a week. They had titles
like *Cold Blooded Revenge* and *From Death to Death* and
Who Killed The Boss? and *The Crippled Snout*. When Josl
read his detective novels, he was utterly immersed in them.
Nothing else existed. He read after work, and he read in the
evening before bed. He read all day when he was on
holidays. He belonged to three libraries in different areas,
and there were never fewer than half a dozen unread
detective novels in the house.

When Lola was fourteen and beginning to read serious
fiction, she had asked Josl why he read such rubbish.

'It keeps my mind off things,' he had answered.

Lola had asked her mother the same question. 'Why does
Dad read such garbage?' she had asked.

'It keeps his mind off things,' Renia had replied.

Lola had a very vague idea of what it was that Josl was

keeping his mind off, and she was too frightened to enquire further. She was already frightened enough about her parents' past. She had grown up with all kinds of phrases spinning around in her head, like 'you don't know what it means to suffer' and 'you don't know the meaning of trouble' and 'you think this is trouble?' and 'you think this is a tragedy?' Lola didn't want to ask any more questions. She didn't want to know what real trouble was.

'If it takes your mind off things, then go and dance, and dance in good health,' Josl had said to Genia.

With the phone off the hook, Genia practised and practised. She was learning the part of Odile in *Swan Lake*. She was rehearsing the ballroom scene in the third act.

She had mastered the mime and the movements when Odile tries to force the prince to marry her. Her arabesques were balancing nicely, but she was having trouble with her fouettés. Her teacher, Marilyn Warner, had told her that she was too old to attempt fouettés. Genia had felt depressed when Miss Warner said this. Genia told Esther, who always rang her after her classes.

'Look, Mum, maybe you could learn another role, or maybe Miss Warner could choreograph the part differently for you,' Esther had suggested.

'I'm only having trouble with my spotting,' Genia had said to her daughter. 'When you do fouettés, you are spinning around and around on one leg, and you have to spot while you are spinning. Spotting stops you from being dizzy when you turn. Your eyes should be the last thing to leave the front of the stage, and the first part of your body to return. You have to turn your body first, then move your head quickly around so that it gets to the front again before the rest of your body,' Genia had explained to Esther.

Now Genia wasn't spotting properly, and she was feeling dizzy. Her back hurt and her feet ached. She could hardly move her shoulders. She felt nauseous. She sat down.

She closed her eyes to stem the dizziness. She saw her

mother's face. Mania Buchbinder's face was full of pride. 'Remember, Genia darling, when Olga Ramanova said you would be a beautiful Giselle?'

'Yes, Mama,' said Genia. 'I remember.'

Genia stood up and took a deep breath. She threw herself into a fouetté. She spun around and around and around. She had known that she could do it.

Every Death

Renia Bensky read the obituary columns of the *Age* and the *Herald* every day. The death notices were the first thing she turned to in the *Jewish News* when it arrived on Fridays.

She read every death. She knew who had died and who they had left behind. She could guess the age of the deceased. She knew if the dead were good or bad people, and whether they had many friends. She knew when they were dearly loved, or when their death notice was only a formal acknowledgement.

Renia could feel the levels of grief behind the announcements. She could detect the pain or anguish or anger behind these public notices.

Every day there were families left without a mother, and families who had lost a father. Every day there were small children left fatherless and motherless. Every day a child died. Many times Renia would see that a husband had given up and died a few months after his wife's death. There were also quite a few wives who didn't want to live without their husbands.

Fathers and mothers and sons and daughters, and even brothers and sisters, wrote poems for the dead. Such touching poems. They were bad verses, but Renia was always touched by the depth of pain and sadness, and the great effort it took to put this into a poetic form.

Renia was scathing about the death notices that came in

large boxed advertisements. She scoffed at the ads that
began 'The Managing Director and the Staff of'.

'Mr Bigshot, Mr Important!' she would say out loud.

Renia often wondered why it was so hard for these
notices to say how very much someone was loved. People
tried, but always came up with the same half a dozen
sentiments. The same neatly packed phrases at the end of a
notice. The announcements usually ended with 'Forever In
Our Hearts', or 'Will Be Sadly Missed By All Who Knew
Him', or 'Forever In Our Thoughts'. Why was it so hard to
write out a scream, or an ache, or a cry of pain?

Renia had never buried anyone she had loved. She had
never written a death notice. In the ghetto, Josl had carried
their stillborn son to the cemetery, but there had been too
many bodies waiting to be buried, and Josl had had to leave
the baby. Renia had stayed in bed. She had been too sick to
walk to the cemetery. Renia wasn't sure exactly how her
mother and father and her four brothers and three sisters
had died. She knew that her mother and two of her sisters had
died in Auschwitz. Her last image of them was of the three
of them walking towards the gas chambers. Her mother was
holding Renia's niece Hanka by the hand.

Renia had often wondered who had knocked her on the
head and pushed her out of the queue for the gas chambers.
Was it a Kapo? Was it a fellow prisoner? Was it a member
of the Gestapo? She never knew.

Renia had heard several conflicting reports about the
deaths of her father and brothers. After the war, she heard
that Jacob had died in Bergen-Belsen, and that Felek had
been shipped to Mathausen and was shot when he tried to
jump off the train. Someone said that Abramek and Shimek
and Renia's father, Israel, died in Dachau. But there was no
conflict about the fact that they were all dead.

In 1972, when the passengers on an American plane were
taken hostage in Lebanon, Renia Bensky was beside herself. The news almost paralysed her. She couldn't read. She

couldn't talk on the phone. She sat in her kitchen all day, and waited for the radio news bulletins. Nothing could distract her from the fate of the hostages. Genia Pekelman said to Ada Small, 'I think Renia has lost her mind.' When Renia knew that the hostages had been released, she rang Lola.

Lola was twenty-five. She was so overweight that even her face had doubled in size. She was wearing a long, blue, voluminous, flower-patterned dress. Lumps of mashed pumpkin had dried on her cuffs. Lola was sitting in her kitchen looking at a huge bucket of nappies soaking in Milton solution. It was ten o'clock at night.

'Lola, darling, I hope I didn't wake you,' Renia said. 'I want to tell you what you should do if you would be one day hijacked on an airplane. First of all you must never say you are Jewish. If anyone should ask you why you are born in Germany, just say it is because you are Polish. Say that your Polish parents went for a holiday to Germany after the war. You see, Lola, Jews who survived the camps were, a lot of them, in Germany after the war.'

Lola was used to calls like this. 'Wouldn't it be easier if I said I was German?' she asked.

'Yes, maybe you are right,' Renia agreed. 'Yes, maybe you are right. And see, Lola, how handy it will be that you did study German at school. You can say a few words in German to the hijackers. In Auschwitz, quite a few times I was saved because I had such good German.'

'You know, Mum,' Lola said, 'I don't think anyone would even ask me if I was Jewish. I've got an Australian passport. Why would they ask me?'

'Oh, Lola,' wailed Renia Bensky, 'You know nothing. The Jews are the first ones they will kill. Look, it happened already, I think the American soldier the hijackers did kill was a Jew. Everybody wants to kill the Jews first, Lola. But what do you know? You grew up a free child in a free country. You know, Lola, maybe it is not so bad that you didn't marry somebody Jewish. Rodney is so blond, and the baby is blond, and they've both got blue eyes. The hijackers would never think the baby is Jewish. Anyway, Lola darling, I shouldn't hold you up. Give the baby a big kiss from me. You sound a bit tired, so try and get an early night.'

Lola put the phone down. The bits of shit had come off the nappies and floated to the top of the bucket. She thought her mother was getting confused. Wasn't it another group of terrorists who had shot the Jew first? She would ask Rodney. She put the nappies in the washing machine.

The next day Renia rang the Immigration Department to ask if they could remove the entry on Lola's passport listing Germany as her place of birth. Renia was switched from one clerk to another. Nobody seemed to understand why this was so important, and nobody could give her an answer.

Renia wrote to the department. Her neighbour, Mr Spratt, checked her letter for her and told her that it was an excellent letter. The Immigration Department replied that if Renia came in to discuss the matter, it would be considered. Renia thought that she would go in with Lola. After all, Lola could talk anybody into anything.

'Mum,' said Lola, 'I'm having enough trouble staying alive in one place. I feel in such a mess. I can't even think about the danger of having Germany as my place of birth in my passport when I travel.'

Renia felt angry. Lola had always disappointed her. It was as if Lola was going out of her way to make sure that she never gave her mother any pleasure. The only thing that Renia had ever asked of Lola was that she be slim. She had been putting Lola on diets for over twenty years. But somehow, despite all the diets, despite all the lettuce and tomatoes, despite the Ryvita biscuits, the thin-trim wafers, the Metracal drink, the sugarless chewing gum and the calorie-less lollies, Lola had always been fat.

Lola had completed slimming courses at Silhouette, the

Elsternwick Weight Loss Clinic, the YWCA gymnasium and Weight Watchers. And she had remained fat.

Renia rang up her local Member of Parliament, Mr Charles. Mr Charles lived around the corner from the Benskys. Renia made a point of always saying hello to him. She also let him know that she voted for him. Mr Charles would help her with the Immigration Department.

Renia was elated the day that Josl picked up Lola's new passport. Next to 'place of birth' was a nice, cream-coloured space.

'Couldn't this make the hijackers suspicious?' asked Topcha Rosen. 'After all,' she continued, 'everyone has a place of birth on a passport. Maybe they will wonder why this girl has nothing next to her place of birth? Anyway, don't worry, Renia. The main thing is not to worry about it. You'll worry Lola, and then she'll be worried, and the hijackers will see a worried person, and they will wonder why the person should be so worried.'

Renia knew that Topcha knew what it was to be worried. And what it was to be in danger. Topcha had been hidden in a bunker in Poland for five years. Topcha's family had shared the bunker with another family. Fifteen people living in a bunker for five years. The bunker was twelve feet by eight feet. They couldn't all lie down at once. They had to roster sleeping hours.

After the war, Topcha's parents couldn't walk. Their muscles had atrophied. Topcha's father never learnt to walk again. Every day, Topcha's brother had gone out to the forests to buy and scavenge food. Topcha's father had built the bunker in 1933. All his friends had laughed at him. When Poland was invaded, he had taken the family's jewels and furs to the bunker. By the end of the war, the family had nothing left to sell. Another few weeks and they would have perished.

Renia also read reports of car accidents in the *Age*. If there was an extra large crash, she also bought the *Sun*, which always had more details. Renia wept for the car-accident victims. She scoured the articles for information. She learnt which streets and which intersections in Melbourne were the most dangerous. She learnt which times of day car accidents were likely to happen. Twilight was a bad time. She learnt that Volvos and Mercedes stood up well in accidents and that, on the whole, the bigger the car, the less damage was likely to be caused to its occupants.

'Drive carefully,' Renia said to Josl every morning. 'Drive carefully,' Renia, Lola and Lina Bensky chorused when they farewelled friends. 'Drive carefully,' the two Bensky daughters said to their husbands whenever the husbands drove anywhere. 'Drive carefully. Drive carefully,' they repeated several times. 'Drive carefully. Drive carefully.' The Bensky women sang it like a mantra.

When Lola was sixteen, she had a boyfriend who was a tow-truck driver. For the Benskys, this young man's other defects paled into insignificance next to the fact that he was a tow-truck driver. The Benskys didn't complain about his long hair, they ignored his tattoos, and they overlooked the fact that he wasn't Jewish.

The tow-truck driver and Lola went out in his tow-truck. They went to the pictures, they went for walks, and they went for drives in the country. When the tow-truck driver brought Lola home after these outings, the tow-truck would come screaming to a halt, late at night, outside the Benskys' bedroom window. Josl and Renia would have to get up and have a cup of hot milk and honey to soothe themselves after Lola's return. 'Jesus, why do you always have to wait up for me?' Lola would ask.

On Lola's eighteenth birthday, the Benskys bought her a large pink Valiant.

'Lola darling,' Renia said, 'We are giving you this car, not because you have been such a wonderful daughter that you deserve a new car, but because we want you to drive in something safe. I want to sleep at night, and so does Daddy. And now you won't have to drive in somebody's old bomb.' Renia loudly emphasized the last 'b' in bomb.

Lola had corrected her mother many times. 'Mum, you don't sound the "b" at the end of bomb. It's like bum. It's pronounced bom.'

Renia always had the same reply. 'So, you are so clever, my Lola, that you are now teaching me English? When you are clever enough to not go out in the old bombs, then I will listen to your English lessons.'

By the time she had her pink Valiant, Lola was no longer with the tow-truck driver. She was going out with an African. He was the blackest man she had ever seen. His name was Abu.

The Benskys and their 'company' prided themselves on their lack of prejudice. Josl often said to his daughter and to his friends, 'After the discrimination that we Jews did suffer, we should have only tolerance and understanding towards anybody in a minority, and towards all races and all religions.' The whole group agreed with Josl.

All of the Benskys' friends had different suggestions for splitting up Lola and Abu.

'Just be firm,' said Izak Pekelman. 'Tell her that you won't put up with it and that's final.'

Genia Pekelman had the best solution. 'Send her to Israel straight away.'

From the moment she arrived, Lola hated Israel. She was contemptuous of the young American Jews who had migrated there. When they asked her if she didn't feel that this was her grass, her earth, her sky, here in Israel, she said she had never been fond of the outdoors. Lola thought that they were all running away from something.

The Jews in Israel didn't look like real Jews to Lola. She had thought that Israel would be full of Aunty Genias and Uncle Izaks. She had thought that she would be greeted by everybody as a long-lost relative. Instead, people had a brusque manner and didn't feel any more affectionately towards her because she was Jewish. Here, everyone was Jewish.

In Israel, perfect strangers asked Lola why she didn't lose weight. A man in the bus one day looked at her and said: 'Young girl, it is lucky that you have such a nice face. Why are you so fat?' A woman in the supermarket offered her the Israeli Army Diet.

After three months in Israel, Lola was very happy to be back home in Melbourne. She was a bit upset when she found out that Abu had gone back to Nigeria. He hadn't written to say that he was going. The Benskys' friends congratulated Renia and Josl on a mission successfully completed.

Renia Bensky always expected the unexpected. She tried to predict the unpredictable. She liked to be prepared for all possibilities, and to be one step ahead of whatever lay in the future.

The perfectly normal, the absolutely routine, always took Renia by surprise. She gasped with horror or disbelief if anyone caught a cold. She then rushed into overdrive. This was an emergency. She bought high-dosage vitamin C tablets before they were fashionable. She made inhalation clinics in the bathroom. She would fill the basin with eucalyptus oil and turn on the two hot-water taps in the shower. The patient had to sit in this steam three times a day.

As well as this, Renia squeezed dozens of oranges and ran around dispensing the juice. She took the victim's temperature every hour. She made extra chicken soup. Josl and the girls joked, when Renia was out of the room, that if the cold didn't kill them, they might just drown in chicken soup.

Some of Lola's most pleasant childhood memories were of being nursed through a cold by Renia. All Renia's anger seemed to dissipate. The harsh looks she often gave Lola were gone. She was soft and sympathetic. She no longer focused on Lola's diet. 'Eat up,' she urged.

All the Benskys' friends could rely on Renia to look after them when they were sick. She visited them. She shopped for them. She rang twice a day to enquire after their progress. She was full of love for them.

In the Lodz ghetto, Renia had found her school friend, Raisl, lying in Palacowa Street. Raisl's face was covered in blood. Renia knew it was tuberculosis. She carried Raisl the four blocks to her apartment. Josl's parents and brother, who shared a room with Renia and Josl, were horrified. They told Renia that Raisl had to be put back in the street.

'Let her at least have a few hours' sleep,' Renia pleaded. Renia cleaned Raisl up and tucked her into her own bed. Raisl kept coughing blood.

Suddenly there was a great commotion outside. It was another raid, another round-up of Jews to be transported out of the ghetto for 'a better life'. Renia, Josl and his parents were trapped. They had no time to run anywhere. Up until then they had been lucky. Josl had a cousin in the Judenrat who had managed to tip them off when a raid was due on Palacowa Street.

Josl's father, Shimek, looked defeated. Josl pushed the four of them into a small cupboard. They all knew it was no use. The SS had dogs. They were done for.

A few minutes later, the door was bashed in by an SS officer. He took one look at Raisl and fled. The SS, Josl's father later laughed, were such cowards. They were terrified of contagious diseases.

The next morning Raisl was dead. Renia walked beside Raisl's body, in the cart that picked up the unclaimed dead, and said Kaddish for Raisl.

Renia bought four loaves of bread a day for the birds in her garden. She bought rye, white sliced, wholemeal and vienna. She walked to Acland Street to get the best bread.

She always had plenty of bread in the house. The few stories about Renia's past that she shared with Lola were about bread. She used to say, 'Lola darling, you don't know what it is to be without bread.' Renia was often eating the toasted rye with caraway seed that she loved when she told this to Lola. 'You know, Lola, there were some people in the ghetto who killed people so that they could have their bread. Mrs Berg, my high-school teacher, didn't report the death of her daughter. She kept the body with her for two weeks so she could claim her daughter's rations. Finally, the neighbours couldn't bear the smell and told the authorities.

'I, myself, one day was carrying my bread ration home. I was stupid and was holding the bread in my hand. A young boy did snatch the bread from me. I ran and ran after him. I did catch him, but he had already gobbled my bread while he was running. He was only about eight years old. His stomach was swollen from starvation. I couldn't even cry for my bread.'

Sometimes, at night, Lola was woken by her mother's nightmares.

'Mama,' Mrs Bensky would call out. 'Mama. Mama. Mama.'

Even when she was little, Lola knew that her mother was not just in the world of sleep. She knew that Renia Bensky was in another world, in another time, with another family.

Lola suspected that this family that her mother was joined to in her nightmares was her mother's real family.

When Lola was seventeen she had crept into the Benskys' bedroom, late one night, to get her alarm clock from their sideboard. Renia and Josl were fast asleep.

As Lola picked up the clock, it slipped from her hand and fell to the ground. Mrs Bensky jumped from her bed. Her eyes were wild. 'Go on, kill me!' she shouted. 'Go on, I don't care what you do to me. Kill me. Kill me.'

Josl woke Renia up gently. He calmed her down. 'It's all right, my darling. It was just a bad dream. Everything is all right. Go back to sleep.'

When Renia was asleep again, Josl went to find his daughter. Lola was in the bathroom washing herself. She had locked the door.

Josl called out to her: 'I am sorry, darling, but when your Mum goes to sleep she can't get away from the past. As soon as she shuts her eyes, she is back again. Are you all right?'

'Yes, I'm fine,' Lola answered. She finished washing her legs and her feet. Her bowels had given in to the shock. She had shat herself.

Renia sat in her kitchen drinking a cup of black tea with cloves. Today the *Herald* was very good. There were two very good death notices today. They both had wonderful quotations. 'Death surprises us in the middle of our hopes,' Mr Jack Lane's wife had put at the end of the notice of her husband's death. And at the end of another notice was: 'Death borders upon our birth, and our cradle stands in the grave.'

The *Jewish Times*, which came from Sydney, also had a very nice death notice this week:

His life was gentle and the elements
So mixed in him that Nature might stand up
And say for all the world, 'This was a Man.'

Renia had heard that the editor of the *Jewish Times* was a very poetic woman.

Renia added these quotes to her notebook of obituary quotations. Her two favourites were: 'A man's dying is more the survivor's affair than his own.' Thomas Mann had written this. And John Donne's beautiful passage, 'Any man's death diminishes me, because I am involved in mankind; and therefore never send to know for whom the bell tolls; it tolls for thee.'

Renia folded the *Herald* and put it away. She had to prepare dinner. Josl liked to eat at 5 p.m. She thought that she would just ring Lola quickly before she began the dinner. Genia had told Renia yesterday that Malka Frenkel had lost three stone at the Jenny Craig Weight Loss Centre. This was not the first good report that Renia had received about the Jenny Craig Centre. She'd heard that Nusia's friend Fela had lost two stone, and that Topcha's daughter, who had always been a big fatty, was now thin. Renia walked to the telephone and dialled Lola's number.

The Holiday

It was the holiday in Olinda, they all agreed, that marked the beginning of the end. Mr and Mrs Bensky, Mr and Mrs Small, Mr and Mrs Pekelman, Mr and Mrs Ganz and Mr Berman had been a group for thirty-two years. 'Our company', they called themselves. Every Easter and every Christmas they went somewhere together.

At first the holidays were modest. They were all migrants, newly arrived refugees, when they met in Australia. They met in the summer of 1950, at Solly Nadel's Guest House in Hepburn Springs. Mr and Mrs Bensky had arrived at Nadel's on a truck. Mrs Bensky and Lola had travelled in the cabin with the driver, and Mr Bensky was strapped to a chair on the back of the truck.

Josl Bensky had paid Jack, the driver, to drive them to Hepburn Springs. In two weeks, Jack would come and pick them up and take them home. The return trip cost Josl five shillings. Mrs Bensky had wept all the way there. She was sure her Josl was going to fall off the truck. And Lola, unnerved by Mrs Bensky's cries, had screamed all the way to Hepburn Springs.

When they arrived, Mr Bensky had had to wait for Jack to unstrap him. He felt a bit humiliated when a group of guests gathered to watch.

It was the Benskys' first holiday in Australia. Mrs Bensky entered Lola in the fancy-dress competition. From some

77

cardboard and newspaper and glue, and a bottle of black ink, Mrs Bensky made Lola a witch's outfit. A black pointed hat, a black fringed cloak and a big false nose. Little Lola, the witch, won second prize.

By the end of the fortnight the 'company' had been formed. Mr and Mrs Bensky, Mr and Mrs Small, Mr and Mrs Pekelman, Mr and Mrs Ganz and Mr and Mrs Berman had gone for walks together after dinner at night. They had bottled the mineral water from the springs together. They had eaten together. They were firm friends.

Mr and Mrs Pekelman had arrived in Melbourne only four weeks earlier. Mrs Bensky took Mrs Pekelman under her wing. She introduced her to Mrs Papov and to Mrs Berg. It was essential, Renia Bensky explained to Genia Pekelman, to be on the good side of these gossip-mongers.

Later, in Melbourne, Renia took Genia shopping. The two women bought a length of black knitted fabric from the Victoria Market. From this material, Renia made two tops with scooped necklines and three-quarter sleeves, and two straight skirts.

Renia made a whole wardrobe for herself and Mrs Pekelman. The total cost of this wardrobe was less than the price of one dress at Myers. Mrs Bensky felt very proud of herself. Mrs Pekelman was grateful, and she remained in eternal admiration of Mrs Bensky.

The two women looked so stylish, so elegant, so beautiful in their new clothes. Mrs Bensky's hair was cut in the new, chic, short, gamin style. She had taught Mrs Pekelman how to roll her thick auburn hair into a chignon. Both women were olive-skinned and strong-limbed. Looking at them, it was impossible to believe that five years ago Renia Bensky was in Auschwitz and Genia Pekelman was in Bergen-Belsen.

At Solly Nadel's Guest House, the men (and an occasional woman) sat inside and played cards. One hundred and two degrees Fahrenheit, and they sat with the windows closed, the air thick with cigarette smoke. And they played cards. They played Red Aces, poker and gin rummy.

The women sat in small groups outside. They chatted to each other and fussed around their own children and other people's children. Shouldn't little Johnny be wearing a sun hat? How could Harry's mother let him out without some sunburn cream on his nose? And look at that Layla, didn't Mrs Hersh know that a young girl shouldn't be allowed to get so fat? And the Horowitz boy, he was already out of control. What would it be like when he was a teenager? For the women on holiday, here at Solly Nadel's in Hepburn Springs, these were the questions of the day.

At night there was dancing. The guests at Solly Nadel's could be divided into six categories. The good dancers, the bad dancers and the non-dancers, and the good card-players, the bad card-players and the non-card-players.

The good dancers enjoyed the highest status at Solly Nadel's. Their importance could only be surpassed by a professor or a doctor. There were not too many professors or doctors at Solly Nadel's, so the good dancers were the élite.

'Look at that Mr Gruner, what a dancer,' Genia Pekelman said almost every morning at the breakfast table. 'He dances the tango and the foxtrot like he was in a world championship of dancing.' Genia Pekelman, who was awkward in the kitchen and around the dinner table, turned into a light-footed, delicate slip of a girl on the dance floor. All her self-consciousness left her. She side-stepped and back-stepped. She whirled in neat, graceful circles. She swivelled her hips and held her head at a coquettish angle.

During the day, the ballroom at Solly Nadel's was used as a dining room. Breakfast, lunch and dinner were served there. At meal times the noise was deafening. One hundred and twenty people ate and talked simultaneously. They ate while they talked. They talked over the top of one another. If they felt they weren't being heard, they shouted. Some of the guests shouted everything they said. The same conversations were repeated every day. The sentiments that were voiced were interchangeable among the guests. Mrs Bloom would probably be saying the same thing as Mrs Fink, and Mrs Freedman's thoughts often echoed Mrs Rose's.

Slivers of sentences shot through the room like crossfire. 'How old is little Esther? Oh, she's not talking yet? My Johnny says many words. And Esther is still in nappies? What a shame. Johnny says for quite a few weeks already, "I need pishy. I need cucky."'

Most of the men were looking for ways to better them-selves. The same conversations travelled from table to table. 'Did you hear that Mr Brown was looking for a good tailor? You can get a job at the Renee of Rome Factory. He doesn't pay so good, but he always gives the Jews work. Watch out for Mr Sal. Never do piecework for him. He complains about every garment.'

Every summer Solly Nadel employed Mr Muller, an elderly Austrian baker, to bake bread. Mr Muller worked seven days a week in December and January. He baked from 5 a.m. to 5 p.m. He baked rye bread, pumpernickel and vienna, and he baked special challah rolls for dinner.

There was never any bread left on the tables after the meals. Mr Grossman saved the leftover bread from his table. After two weeks, he took home three cardboard boxes of bread. Other people did the same.

'He is a peasant, that Mr Grossman,' said Mrs Lipshutz. Frieda Factor interrupted her. 'We should understand, Mrs Lipshutz, that this is not his normal behaviour. I don't know if you know this, Mrs Lipshutz, but Mr Grossman was in Mathausen concentration camp.' 'Well, he is now in Melbourne, Australia, where there is plenty of bread,' Mrs Lipshutz replied. 'That sort of behaviour causes anti-Semitism,' she added.

Mrs Lipshutz, who had been in Australia for ten years, was not happy with the postwar influx of Jews. 'They are a different brand of Jew altogether,' she told her Australian neighbour, Mrs Cunningham. 'They are peasants. We, Adam and I, came from cultured families. We read books, we went to the theatre, we went to the opera, we always had the best seats. We travelled in Europe. My father spoke fluent French. We were not peasants. You will see, these Jewish refugees will make the Australian people into anti-Semites.'

'Oh, no, Mrs Lipshutz,' said Mrs Cunningham. 'I feel so sorry for some of them. They're still young girls. With those numbers on their arms they remind me of branded cattle. And Mrs Lipshutz, I met a young woman who was a dentist in Warsaw before the war, and now she is a cleaner. And her sister, who was a doctor, is working as a machinist.'

'Pheh!' said Mrs Lipshutz. 'They all say that they were doctors in Poland.'

Later that night, Mrs Lipshutz told Mr Lipshutz that her greatest fears had been confirmed. Mrs Cunningham, their hard-working, church-going neighbour, had told her that these new Jewish migrants looked like cattle.

If it was so easy for a good, kind person like Mrs Cunningham to be an anti-Semite, said Morry Lipshutz, what hope was there for the world?

The company went to Solly Nadel's for their Christmas holidays every year until 1959. By then they had a bit more money. Things were looking up for most of the group. The Smalls and the Pekelmans were partners in a knitting factory. Mr Bensky owned Joren Fashions, a small factory that manufactured ladies' suits. Costumes, Josl called them. Pola and Moishe Ganz already had six machinists working for them at Champs Elysees Blouses, and Mr Berman wholesaled plastic bags. Joseph Zelman was the wealthiest of the group. He was already building his sixth block of flats. He bought the land, built the flats, and sold them as they were being built. He worked day and night. He undercut his competition by settling for a smaller profit. In 1959 he was on his way to banking his first million.

In 1959 the company went to Surfers Paradise. They rented four units in the same block in Cavill Avenue. Mrs Bensky brought her own frozen chicken stock. Mrs Zelman brought six pounds of lean beef, which she made into three big klops on the first day. One klops for lunch, and two for later in the week. Mrs Ganz stewed a big pot of apples and baked a sponge cake, and everyone felt at home.

They ate their meals outside, around the swimming pool. At night they walked along the beach. For Mr Bensky, the highlight of this holiday was the matzoh brei that Mrs Zelman made for everyone most mornings. Josl was the first at the breakfast table each morning. He looked so happy eating the matzoh brei that Mrs Zelman thought she could have happily made it for him forever. Some men, she thought, are so easy to please.

Surfers Paradise, the company decided, was a very successful holiday place. They went there often after that.

The company had other memorable holidays. They went to Rotorua in New Zealand. They had mud baths and mineral spas. Mrs Bensky loved this. She sat happily for hours covered in hot mud. Josl had to be ordered into the mud. He hated it. On the second day Josl sprained his ankle, and had to spend the rest of his New Zealand holiday doing what he liked best. He lay on the bed in the motel room and read detective novels. He finished a book and a box of chocolates a day.

Mrs Ganz and Mr Zelman went to the mineral baths together. Mrs Bensky was worried. She feared that the attachment between them was more than it should be. No-one else appeared worried.

In New Zealand the company discovered duty-free shopping. All the families came home with new cameras.

In 1982 the company went to Israel. They had planned this trip for months. Mr Bensky was in charge of the itinerary. They stopped in Las Vegas on their way to Israel.

Mr Bensky was one of the keenest card-players of the group. He loved to gamble. Mr Zelman and Mr Pekelman thought that Las Vegas wasn't really on the way from Melbourne to Tel Aviv, but they kept their thoughts to themselves.

Josl Bensky was deliriously happy in Las Vegas. He lost at blackjack, he lost at roulette. He lost playing chemin de fer and five card stud poker. He played the poker machines in the main gambling hall, and he played the mini poker machines in the toilets. In two days Josl Bensky lost $700. 'Las Vegas', he told everyone in Melbourne when he got back, 'was the best part of the trip.'

'There's too many Jews here for me,' said Izak Pekelman in Israel. 'I don't feel so good among so many Jews.' The rest of the group thought that what Izak said may have sounded a little strange but, in different ways, they all knew what he meant.

Renia Bensky stayed in the hotel room with the 'flu for most of their three weeks in Israel. Genia Pekelman wouldn't go to the pictures, or to the theatre, or to any concerts. 'If it's all the same to you,' she said, 'I would prefer to stay in the hotel. It makes me too nervous to be with a crowd.' To her husband Genia said what the others had understood she was trying to say: 'Izak, I can't stand being in the middle of so many Jews. It makes me too nervous. What if someone starts to shoot at us? It reminds me too much of too many things.'

George Small couldn't eat anything in Israel. 'This is not what we ate at home in Poland,' he said. 'This is the food of Arabs, not the food of Jews.'

In Mea Shearim, the Orthodox area of Jerusalem, Josl Bensky bellowed: 'Who do they think they are, these Orthodox? What are they doing? Why do they have to draw such attention to themselves? Where in the Talmud does it say you have to wear such a long black coat, and the short black trousers, and the black hats? This is the modern world, not the old world. Stupid bastards. They cause trouble for everyone. Haven't the Jews had enough trouble?' By now Josl was almost in tears.

That night the company were having dinner in Jerusalem. A group of Orthodox young men came and sat at the next table. Josl looked at them and said loudly, 'Oy, I'm going to vomit.'

Mr Berman liked Israel. But Chaim Berman was a quiet man. He always agreed with the majority. He kept to himself the elation that he felt at being in the homeland of the Jewish people. He loved the robustness of the people, the honesty, the lack of artifice. He loved the commitment and the loyalty. Chaim thought that it was a privilege to live for an ideal, and in Israel people were living for an ideal. They had, Chaim Berman thought, something more valuable than central heating and new television sets.

Pola Ganz had hoped that she would be able to find Chaim Berman a new wife in Israel, but after a few days Pola decided that a Jewish woman from Melbourne might be more suitable.

'You have to be careful with these Israelis,' she said to Ada Small. 'We wouldn't want to find Chaim a wife who married him because he owns a nice house and a good business in Australia.'

Ada Small agreed that they had to be careful.

The group visited a kibbutz in the Negev. They all loved the kibbutz. They were very impressed by the size of the kitchen, and the laundry facilities. 'Did you ever see such a stove in your life?' said Joseph Zelman. With all his blocks of flats, Joseph knew about kitchens.

'Australia is paradise,' Josl Bensky said on their last night in Israel. He raised his glass and proposed a toast to Australia. 'To Australia,' they all chorused.

In Israel, Renia Bensky had become increasingly agitated about Pola Ganz and Joseph Zelman. Several times, she thought, she had caught them looking at each other tenderly.

By the time she was back in Australia, Renia Bensky was sure there was a heat between Pola Ganz and Joseph Zelman. And Renia Bensky felt hot watching them.

'Poor Mina Zelman,' Renia said to Josl. 'She hasn't

suffered enough? It wasn't enough what she did go through in Bergen-Belsen? Now she has to have a Romeo for a husband? And what about poor Moishe Ganz? Maybe he is not so intelligent as our dear Joseph Zelman, but he has always been a first-class husband to Pola. The trouble with Pola is that she doesn't know when she's got something good. She is always looking for something new. She says to me, "Oh Renia, I've found a new hairdresser. Oh Renia, I've found a new dressmaker. Oh Renia, this manicurist is better and cheaper." Now, whatever Joseph Zelman has got in his trousers is something Pola Ganz thinks is better than what she's got at home.'

Renia knew that after the war there were strange and hasty alliances formed. Women married for security. Men married mothers. Strangers married strangers. People were starved of comfort, companionship and affection. Odd matches were made. There was not always time to wait for love.

Young girls married older men. Students married their teachers. Neighbours and cousins got married. Everyone was in a hurry to begin a normal life.

Dead wives, dead husbands and dead children were present at many of these marriage ceremonies.

Renia decided that something had to be done about Pola and Joseph. She hired a private detective. Two weeks later, the private detective gave Renia a photograph of Joseph Zelman sitting in his car outside Pola Ganz's house. Renia felt very pleased with herself.

It was Easter, and the company went to Olinda. Renia packed the photograph carefully at the bottom of her suitcase. She hadn't told Josl about the detective.

In Olinda, it seemed as though it was going to be another nice Easter break. The group settled into their holiday routine. They ate nice big breakfasts, they went for walks, they sat in the autumn sun.. They had good lunches, a nap after lunch, another small walk and it was time for dinner. After dinner they played cards. After three days they were all in good spirits, and felt invigorated by the country air.

On Sunday night, Renia showed Ada Small the photograph. Ada didn't say much. 'Why have you got a photograph of Joseph in his car?' she asked. Renia explained the location of the photograph, and its implication.

Ada Small went straight to Pola Ganz. Pola laughed and showed the photograph to Moishe. Moishe looked carefully at the photograph. He didn't say anything. Later, he said to Josl: 'So what, what does that photograph prove? Nothing.' Josl had to agree.

Nobody mentioned the photograph to Mina Zelman. 'She's got enough trouble,' said Ada Small. 'She's so tall. At her height she would never find another husband.'

Pola refused to speak to Renia Bensky. Renia tried to explain that she had done this for Pola's own good, but Pola wouldn't even come near her.

'If she is going to be so unintelligent about this,' Renia said to Josl, 'she can go to hell. I am finished with Pola Ganz.'

The atmosphere became so unpleasant that the company left Olinda a day early.

What was really shocking about all of this, Ada Small said to her manicurist, was that Renia Bensky and Pola Ganz had almost been machatunim. There was no word in English for machatunim, Ada explained. Machatunim was the word for the relationship between a couple's parents-in-law. Renia and Pola were almost the mothers-in-law of each other's children. Renia's daughter Lina had almost married Pola's son, Sam.

There was an unspoken, unanimous decision among the company not to tell the children why they were no longer friends. The children had to be protected.

One of Lina's colleagues at the law firm where she worked told her that she'd heard a rumour that the rift between Renia and Pola was caused by Renia's accusations that Pola had committed adultery with Joseph Zelman.

Sam Ganz laughed when Lina told him. 'My mother,

having an affair? You're joking. She goes to bed in flannel nightgowns and wears face cream, throat cream, neck cream, arm and leg cream. As a kid, I used to watch her hop into bed and wonder why she didn't slip straight out again. There must be another reason Renia and Pola aren't speaking.'

Mrs Zelman also wondered why Renia and Pola weren't speaking. Maybe Mrs Ganz had done something she shouldn't have been doing with Mrs Bensky's Josl. She wouldn't put it past that Pola Ganz to meddle with someone else's husband.

Mr Zelman and Mrs Ganz also stopped speaking to each other. 'He was a rotten lover,' Mrs Ganz said to her sister. 'He wore his socks to bed.'

The company collapsed. Mr Small and Mr Pekelman and Mr Berman met Mr Zelman and Mr Ganz to try and patch things up. They agreed that it was important to forgive and to forget. To make a fresh start. But the women wouldn't budge.

Moishe Ganz believed his wife, and wouldn't hear a word against her. Josl, although he thought that Renia shouldn't have interfered, knew that she didn't do it out of malice.

People took sides. Mr and Mrs Small sided with the Ganzes, and Mr and Mrs Pekelman stayed loyal to the Benskys. Chaim Berman remained friendly with everyone.

For thirty-two years the company hadn't missed a Saturday night at the pictures. Now they stopped going to the pictures. They stopped playing cards. They stopped going out for supper. They stayed at home.

Mr and Mrs Small and Mr Berman took short walks around Caulfield, but their hearts weren't in it. The Zelmans tried to learn bridge, but everyone else at the Herzl Club could play well, and they gave up. Izak Pekelman took up golf. He dropped it a week later.

At weddings, barmitzvahs, engagements and anniversaries and birthdays, people knew to put the Benskys and the Ganzes at different tables.

Genia Pekelman talked separately to Renia and Pola. She begged them to make up. She said to each of them, 'Couldn't you just put this behind you and make a new start?' That approach hadn't worked with Genia's daughter Rachel, and it didn't work with Renia and Pola.

Genia tried again. 'If you can't be friends, at least don't be enemies. Let us all go out together again, and maybe things will get slowly better. And we will be a group again. And people will stop talking about us. And if things are not as good as they look, at least it will look as though they are good.' Genia's mother used to quote this old saying to her. It had a melodic lilt in Yiddish that got lost in the translation. Nothing that Genia Pekelman said moved Renia or Pola.

This was the price of success, thought Genia. This is what happens when you can afford to hire a private detective. Life used to be so straightforward in the old days in Melbourne, thought Genia.

When they first came to Australia, some of them had lived two families to one room. Even the most comfortably off of the group, the Smalls, lived in a room at the back of their factory.

On weekends all their children played together. Now, when Genia reminded Rachel that Jack Zelman was unattached, Rachel replied, 'I hate Jack Zelman.' Rachel and Jack had played together so nicely when they were small.

Genia had thought that she had created cousins for her Rachel and her Esther in Australia. A new family. She thought that the company and their children would regard each other as family. As cousins, aunties, uncles, nephews, nieces. As it turned out, none of their children were friends, except for Lina and Sam. And now the company themselves were no longer friends.

They had all ended up, Genia thought, in the same

position that they had been in in Germany after the war. No family. No close friends. At least they had their children. But the children were another story. Even the children had brought them troubles.

Soon, Genia thought, they would all start dying. And they would die alone. One of Genia's most comforting thoughts had been that she would never have to die alone. Not like the hundreds and hundreds of dead in the streets in the ghetto.

So this is how things had turned out, thought Genia Pekelman. This is how things had turned out in the goldeneh medina, the new world.

The Children

Sam Ganz was the Managing Director of Champs Elysees Blouses. Sam was on the phone negotiating the purchase of a turn-of-the-century musical sideboard. When you opened its glass doors, this sideboard played *Für Elise*. Sam was on the verge of agreeing to pay the asking price when his father walked into the office. 'I'll call you back, and we'll discuss it this afternoon,' Sam said to the antique dealer. 'Just talking to the mechanic about the Volvo. It needs its front brake pads replaced,' he explained to his father.

Moishe Ganz was the Chairman of Eiffel Tower Fashions, which owned Champs Elysees Blouses. Pola and Moishe had set up the business in 1950.

Pola and Moishe had met in Paris, in the Hotel Lutetia, in 1946. They had both just survived the war in Poland – she in hiding, and he in a labour camp. Now they were being looked after at the Hotel Lutetia.

During the war the Hotel Lutetia had been the Gestapo headquarters in Paris. Now it was a welcoming centre for the few Jews who had survived Nazi Europe.

Pola and Moishe had rooms on the same floor at the Lutetia. They began talking to each other. Soon they began to meet in the foyer of the hotel in the mornings. Then they spent their days together.

After two weeks, Moishe proposed to Pola. Pola said: 'No, never! I don't want to get married. I want to live a bit,

91

to grow up. I am twenty-one, and I haven't had any boyfriends. I haven't done many things a normal girl does. I don't know who I am, where I am. I only know I don't want to get married. Not now, never.' 'Never say never,' said Moishe. Three weeks later, Pola and Moishe were married.

They moved out of the Lutetia and into a small bed-sitting room in the Rue de Rennes. Pola and Moishe shared their sixth-floor flat in the Rue de Rennes with a family of dark-brown rats. Pola and Moishe kept their bread, coffee, tea, sugar and even butter wrapped in newspaper, and hung these parcels in pillowcases from a hook on the wall.

One day Pola reached for one of her shoes from the bottom of the cupboard. She surprised a sleeping rat. The rat ran up Pola's arm. Pola wept. The rat had shat on her skirt. 'I knew I shouldn't have got married,' she said to Moishe.

Pola and Moishe did have good times in Paris. They went for long walks along the river. They went to the zoo. Even then, straight after the war, Paris was a city of lovers. Pola and Moishe got to know each other slowly. It was a time of rest and recuperation. A honeymoon of sorts.

They were waiting for their immigration papers to be finalized. Moishe taught Pola to ice-skate. They fed pigeons in the Luxembourg Gardens. They walked arm-in-arm alongside other lovers in the Tuileries and on the Boulevard St Germain.

Years later, when people talked about the beauty of Paris, Pola could only remember the rats.

Baby Sam was born three months before Pola and Moishe were due to leave for Australia. Pola wept with happiness at the birth of her son. The night after Pola had been freed from the cellar in which she had spent the last year of the war, she had had a dream. Her father, who had died in the cellar, had come to her in her dream. 'Pola, my daughter,' he had said, 'you will one day give birth to a son. And this son will have in him all the fathers and all the sons from our family. I will be there in him. Your grandfather will be there. And your grandfather's grandfather. We will all be there. As soon as you see your son, you will see us.'

Sam was a beautiful baby. He had a wise face and a quiet disposition. Pola saw that her father had been right. Sam looked just like him.

Moishe was also in love with Sam. He kissed him hundreds of times a day. When Sam was two months old, Moishe took him to the Punch and Judy show at the Bois de Boulogne. He pointed out dogs and cats and birds in the street. He repeated the Yiddish, French and English words for these animals to Sam. As soon as he had set eyes on Sam, Moishe had seen that Sam was the image of Moishe's mother. Moishe also recognized Sam's eyes: they belonged to his youngest sister, Chana. Chana and her mother had died of tuberculosis in the ghetto.

Moishe had hoped that Sam would be born in Australia. He had gone to the Australian Embassy every day to ask if the visa had been approved. 'I want my child to be born in Australia. I want that he should be very Australian,' Moishe had pleaded. But the process couldn't be hurried.

The Ganzes arrived in Australia in May 1949. They spent the first month at the migrant hostel at Bonegilla. Pola and Sam slept in the women's quarters. Moishe was in the men's dormitory. Pola's bed was in the middle of rows and rows of beds. The toilets were outside. There were no lights at night. Sam wasn't well. He had diarrhoea. At night, Pola changed his nappies in the dark. As soon as she had a clean nappy on him, he had another bout of diarrhoea. Pola had been nervous about coming to Australia. Australia was proving to be worse than her worst fears.

Moishe found a nice room in Brunswick. The Jewish Welfare Agency furnished the room, and the Ganzes moved in. Moishe was happy. Things were looking up.

Pola put on her best dress and went to Georges, the most exclusive department store in Melbourne. She took a pencil and a notepad. In the dressing room of the Ladies Daywear department, Pola sketched half a dozen of the blouses that they had in the store.

Moishe bought some fabric. Together, in their room in Brunswick, Pola and Moishe made copies of the blouses. Moishe got orders for these blouses from several small retailers around Melbourne. Champs Elysees Blouses was in business.

'Mum,' said Sam, 'I've put a deposit on a sideboard. It's antique and it's very beautiful. It will be a good investment. In another few years it will be worth twice what I am paying for it.' 'Good, darling,' said Pola. She liked Sam to be happy.

'It was very expensive,' said Sam. 'But this sideboard is one of a kind. You'd never find another one like it, and it's going to look fabulous in my den. I took Ruth to see it, and she adores it.'

Mrs Ganz, unfortunately, didn't adore Ruth. She thought that Ruth had married Sam to better herself. Ruth came from a poor family. She had adapted herself very well to a moneyed lifestyle. Too well, thought Pola.

'Well, darling, enjoy this sideboard,' said Pola. 'How much did you pay for it? '

'Fifty thousand,' said Sam.

'What, are you crazy? Fifty thousand? Does it have eighteen-carat gold cutlery in the drawers? Are you a meshugana? You are, you are mad.'

Eventually Pola calmed down. It was only money, she thought. Sam was their only son. What did it matter? Nobody was hurt by the purchase. Pola did feel, though, that it would be unwise for Moishe to know that Sam had paid fifty thousand for a sideboard.

When Moishe was angry with Sam, he would call him a 'little prince'. 'He doesn't know what it is to work hard, to earn your own money,' Moishe would say.

Moishe was disappointed in Sam. Not that he voiced this

disappointment. Moishe believed that to air a problem only made the problem seem worse. Sam had been a mediocre student at school, and had failed his matriculation year. The Ganzes had no alternative. They had taken Sam into the business.

Pola and Sam worked out a scheme whereby Sam would pay for the sideboard with three separate cheques. He would tell his father that he was buying three pieces of furniture, not one. Fifty thousand for three pieces would seem reasonable.

Moishe didn't notice Sam's purchases. He had other things on his mind. His two daughters both wanted to leave their husbands. Moishe didn't know what to do.

Last week Debbi, the elder daughter, had told him that she was leaving her husband, Oscar. She was in love, she said, with Adrian Gartener. Moishe didn't see that there was much difference between Oscar and Adrian Gartener. Why Debbi was transferring her love from one to another bewildered Moishe.

'Love, love,' he raged to Pola, 'They all talk about this big word love. It is not "love", but "LOVE". Tell me Pola, can you see that that Adrian Gartener is any more of a mensch than Oscar Kreutzer? They are both pishers.'

Helen, the Ganzes' other daughter, was also looking for fulfilment. She had said to her father, 'Issy is a nice enough person. He's good-hearted and kind to the children, but I can't bear him to touch me. It's not that he wants to touch me so often. Luckily, he is not all that interested. But when he moves towards me in bed I feel sick.'

Pola Ganz knew that Helen had been having an affair with one of her colleagues at the University of Melbourne. She had told Helen to be sure to be absolutely discreet. 'Darling, for a few hot minutes in someone else's bed, you don't throw away a good husband,' she had said to her daughter.

The Ganzes had supported their sons-in-law through

university. Afterwards, they had set them up in business. They had bought Issy a law practice, and Oscar a dental surgery.

Moishe felt tired thinking about his daughters. Moishe had thought that the days of having trouble with his children were over. What was wrong with young people today? They had no stamina. They had to be gratified immediately. Their love life had to be perfect. Their sex had to be the latest up-to-date manoeuvres. If they were not having simultaneous orgasms they looked for another partner.

What about love? And tenderness? And patience? And loyalty? Life, for his children, was too transient to allow for love, thought Moishe.

Pola and Moishe had given their children everything. The children had been spoilt and coddled. Moishe had set up Champs Elysees Blouses one block from Elwood Primary School so that Pola could take hot soup to school at lunchtime for Sam and the girls.

Still, his girls were better than other people's girls, thought Moishe. Look at poor Renia Bensky. Her Lola, who was so clever at school, had refused to go to university. And then she had married a goy. At least, through marriage, thought Moishe, Lola had become a wife and a mother. Before that she had been a hippie. She had walked everywhere, even in Collins Street, barefooted, with bells around her neck and long dirty dresses. Moishe had felt so sorry for Renia Bensky.

And, Moishe thought, his Debbi and Helen were better than Genia Pekelman's Esther. Esther was always preoccupied and distracted. She couldn't finish her sentences. Her anxiety blinded her. Last year she had driven through an amber light and killed an elderly man. She hadn't seen him. Izak and Genia Pekelman had visited the man's family to see if there was anything they could do to help. The family had said that there was nothing that the Pekelmans could do for them. There were no witnesses, and the death was recorded as an accident. Izak made a large donation to the Royal Children's Hospital in the dead man's name.

Sam Ganz had a problem. The price he had agreed to pay for the sideboard was seventy thousand, not fifty thousand. He knew his parents would never understand. They really weren't very educated, thought Sam. They knew nothing about antiques. He had to find twenty thousand dollars.

All Sam's and Ruth's expenditures went through the company's books. That was how Pola knew exactly how much Ruth spent at Figgins and Georges and David Jones every week.

Sam frowned. He would have to find a way to pay the extra twenty thousand dollars. Maybe he could give his friend Solly Rosenberg a cheque for twenty thousand. Sam could tell Moishe that he was buying Solly's computer for a very good price, to use at home. Solly could then write out a cheque for twenty thousand, which Sam could give directly to the antique dealer.

At Champs Elysees Blouses, Sam earned a hundred thousand dollars a year. He also received one-fifth of the company's profits. Sam was a wealthy man, but he felt like a small boy who was not allowed to be in charge of his own pocket money. Sam tolerated this discomfort. Now and then he thought of doing something that interested him more, but he couldn't think of anything.

Every winter Pola and Moishe went to Surfers Paradise for three weeks. Pola went at the beginning of June, and when she came back, three weeks later, Moishe went. They both felt that they couldn't be away from Champs Elysees Blouses at the same time.

'If Sam is the Managing Director, he should be able to manage the factory,' Ada Small often said to the Ganzes. 'Moishe, Sam is thirty-two. He is not a baby. He can look after the business.' But Pola and Moishe both agreed that it would be unwise for them to be away from the factory together.

Every Sunday the Ganz family had lunch together. Sam, Debbi and Helen, their spouses and their children came to Pola and Moishe's house. Pola's housekeeper, Mrs Staub, prepared the food. Pola was one of the few women in their group who had a full-time housekeeper. 'I work all day. Why should I work more when I come home?' Pola would say. She always felt a need to defend her use of a house-keeper. The food that Mrs Staub made was delicious. Pola's friends and Pola's children regarded Mrs Staub's meals as inferior because they were not cooked by Pola.

Today Mrs Staub had prepared gefilte fish, chopped liver, a grated egg and onion salad, a potato salad, roast chicken, and chicken schnitzels for the children, and a salmon patty for Issy.

Issy Segal was a fussy eater. Every day for breakfast Issy had a bowl of Kelloggs cornflakes. He had been having this breakfast for twenty years, since he was ten. For lunch, he had one cheese sandwich. White bread with Havarti cheese. For seventeen years, Issy had had a slice of Kraft cheddar in his sandwich. One day Debbi had said to her brother-in-law, 'Couldn't you try another cheese? A real cheese. That stuff you're eating is plastic. Try Havarti.' Issy did. And now he ate Havarti cheese in his sandwich. Last year, Debbi had suggested Issy try some Jarlsberg cheese in his sandwich. Issy said that he was perfectly happy with Havarti.

Every Sunday Issy picked at his salmon patty. The rest of the family ate heartily. 'This is a very good gefilte fish today,' said Pola. 'Last week you couldn't get Murray Perch in Melbourne. The places that had a Murray Perch were selling them for a fortune. It happens every Pesach. The fish shops save their stocks of Murray Perch for just before Pesach, and then they put up the price. They know that at Pesach they can get double the price.'

'Mum, we can afford to pay a bit more for a Murray Perch,' said Debbi. 'It is easy for you to say that,' said Pola. 'Listen to her,' continued Pola. 'She says "we can afford". Who is this "we" that can afford this? Who is this "we" that has earned the money to pay this price for a Murray Perch? Is it you, my darling daughter?'

Luckily, just at that moment, one of the grandchildren dropped a piece of beetroot onto his white shirt, and everyone was diverted from the issue of who earned the money in this family.

The matter of food took over from the matter of money. Pola, Debbi and Helen all tried to push food into the children.

'Harry, have some chicken.'

'Melanie, please eat the schnitzel before the potato.'

'Jonathan, you have to eat the fish before you can have any salad.'

'Jason, you know that salmon patty belongs to Daddy. Have a chicken wing.'

'Have you had a drink yet?'

'Don't drink the lemonade before you finish your meal.'

'Don't eat so much egg, you'll be sick. Have some potato instead.'

'Eat more egg salad, it's good for you.'

This was the main conversation at the lunch table.

After the meal, Pola and Moishe played with the grand-children, and Debbi and Helen washed the dishes. The sisters had never got on well. They had never confided in each other. Each thought that the other was the favoured daughter. But they had a few things in common. They both wanted to leave their husbands. They both despaired of their brother Sam. And they both hated Ruth.

'Did you see that outfit that Ruth was wearing?' said Helen. 'I saw it in Gucci. It cost three thousand bucks.'

'Three thousand bucks!' said Debbi. 'Jesus, by the time our kids grow up there'll be no money left in the business, the rate that Ruth's going through it. I noticed, too, that she had another new ring. Sam keeps buying her jewellery. First of all Sam bought himself a wife. He did, he bought

Ruth with that car and that big engagement diamond. And now he just keeps paying. He's an imbecile.'

'I wonder what she's got that makes her worth all that expenditure?' said Helen.

Helen contemplated telling her sister about her affair with Malcolm Bourke. Sometimes she longed to be close to her sister, but something prevented her. Helen decided against telling Debbi. Debbi might use the information against her in some way.

Helen knew that her affair with Malcolm Bourke had no future. Malcolm wasn't Jewish, and Helen couldn't imagine being married to a non-Jew. There was a comfort and a familiarity and a trust that she felt when she was with Jews.

Helen had rarely found Jewish men sexy. Standing at her mother's kitchen sink, Helen closed her eyes for a moment. She thought of Malcolm licking her, manipulating her. She thought of Malcolm caressing her buttocks, his head between her legs. Helen had to steady herself. She felt limp.

On the few occasions that she and Issy made love, he left his pyjamas on. Helen would lift her nightie to just above her waist. For three minutes they would be joined in a wordless union.

Helen wondered if she would ever find a Jewish man she couldn't wait to fuck. Would there ever be a Jew that she would lust after? Be hungry for? Feel hot about?

There was Charles Roth. He was their solicitor. He was small, articulate and fiery. He had a spark and a swiftness that Helen found attractive. He wasn't overly concerned with himself. He seemed indefatigable. His enthusiasm was infectious. Charles Roth had put himself through law school by playing the piano in jazz bars at night. Now his law practice was very successful and he was a wealthy man. Charles Roth was, however, married. And happily married, Helen had heard.

Never mind, Helen thought. She would make an effort to meet as many Jewish men as she could. It was better to try and find another husband now than in ten years' time when she would be middle-aged. Anything would have to be better than the brief intertwining of the pyjamas and the nightie.

'It's better that I leave now,' Helen had said when her mother suggested that she wait until the children were older. 'Mum, the kids will be happier if I'm happier. Issy is at the surgery until eight every night. They'll see just as much of him. If I wait until I'm forty, I'll probably have forgotten what it feels like to feel like a real woman.'

'Helen, darling, there is more to a good marriage than a good shtoop. Believe me, I know what I'm talking about,' said Pola Ganz.

Helen and Debbi had finished the dishes.

'Debbi, I'm not happy with Issy,' said Helen. 'Can we have a cup of coffee somewhere tomorrow, and talk?'

'Sure,' said Debbi. 'I'll meet you at The Place at nine.'

Debbi and Helen left Oscar and Issy in the same week.

'Look, Pola,' said Moishe, 'if people are going to talk, let them get all the talking about us over with at the same time. It's better that the girls did it together. Otherwise we would have everybody talking about us this week, and then again everyone talking about us next week, or next month, or next year. Now, they will get double the pleasure in their talking, and we will get it over with at once.'

Pola could see the good sense in that. Everyone in the community would get twice as much joy in the Ganzes' failure as parents, and the Ganzes would only have to endure the humiliation for half the time. Moishe could always see the good side of a bad situation, thought Pola.

'You think, Moishe, that I should speak to Sam about that Ruth?' said Pola. 'I mean, Moishe, if we have to have people talking, and marriages finishing, and grandchildren who are going to suffer, then maybe I should suggest to Sam that he leaves that bitch Ruth. Three divorces wouldn't be any harder than two divorces. We could get a special bulk price from a divorce lawyer. Things couldn't be worse. Sam could be comforted and looked after by his sisters, who would understand exactly what he is going through. What do you think, Moishe?'

Moishe started laughing. He had known Pola for thirty-four years, but her efficiency still surprised him. 'Pola, I think that maybe we should leave the matter of his marriage or his divorce to Sam himself.'

Pola was disappointed, but she knew Moishe was right. Still, Pola couldn't resist making a few enquiries.

'Sammy, my darling, does Ruth cook you the schnitzel the way that you like it?' she said to her son.

Sam looked bewildered. 'No, Mum. Ruth doesn't cook schnitzel. She doesn't fry any foods. She can't bear the frying smell. She says it stays in her hair for hours.'

Pola put her hands over her mouth to keep her response inside her.

Sam was puzzled by his mother's concern about Ruth's cooking. He was glad that Pola was distracted. He needed some peace and quiet. Yesterday Sam had bought a hat stand for ten thousand dollars. It was a beautiful hat stand. This hat stand had cerulean blue ceramic balls at the end of every hook, and a ceramic sculpture of an owl at the base.

Now Sam had to figure out how to pay for the hat stand without the transaction going through Champs Elysees Blouses' books. Sam thought that Pola and Moishe might just be preoccupied enough with the divorces not to question the purchase of another home computer. He could repeat the cheque-swapping routine with Solly Rosenberg.

Moishe was with his solicitor and his accountant. They were trying to organize the family finances so that their assets would be protected in case of financial disputes in the property settlements of their daughters' divorces.

Moishe had a headache. Everything was in joint names,

in trust funds for the children, in trust funds for the grandchildren. They had already had two lawyers and two accountants working on it for a week.

Moishe noticed that Sam had bought himself another computer. Some people are easily pleased, he thought. If only his daughters would settle for another computer.

A Mixed Marriage

From the day that Lola fell in love with another man, her husband smelt bad. The smell was like stale, sweet cheese. It came from his body and hovered in a thick net around the bed. It made Lola feel bilious.

She began sleeping with the window open. For thirty-five years she had lived with deadlocks, combination locks and iron bolts; her home security system was updated annually. Now, her fear of rapists, burglars and murderers paled next to the horror of the smell.

It came from his ears, his feet, his hands and his neck. She could smell it in the bathroom when he showered. In the kitchen, it crept across the breakfast table. It soaked into her coffee and filtered itself through her grapefruit juice.

Was Rodney suspicious? Was this his body's reaction? Like a skunk putting out a stink when it feels in danger?

But Rodney didn't know that she was in love with anyone but him. She had been devotedly faithful to him for thirteen years. More than that, they were the ideal couple. Lola loved the image of herself, a dark, wild-haired, large-eyed Jewess, standing next to the tall, pale son of the city's establishment.

The smell lodged itself in Lola's throat. She was unable to eat. She got up and called to her children through the intercom system. 'Kids, we have to leave in five minutes or you'll be late for school.' Lola had never been late for anything. In all her years of psychotherapy, she had not missed one minute of one session. Lola liked to deliver her children to their schools an hour early. This allowed time for possible delays due to heavy traffic, a flat tyre, a mechanical failure or other emergencies. Lola felt that she would be able to tackle any emergency clear-headedly, secure in the knowledge that she would still be on time.

The night before Lola's first day at school, her mother had sat her down for a talk. The family had been in Australia for three years. Mr and Mrs Bensky worked behind sewing machines in a factory during the day, and behind sewing machines at home at night. 'Lolala, my Lolala,' Mrs Bensky said, 'You will be in a school now with Australian children. I want you always to remember that a Jewish boy will make you the best husband. Australian boys, they learn from their fathers to drink beer and to smack their wives. My Lolala, what do you know what it is to be smacked? To be treated worse than a dog?'

Lola couldn't imagine anyone smacking the beautiful Mrs Bensky. She knew that the Nazis had. They had tattooed a number on Mrs Bensky's slender strong arm. Lola told anyone who asked that this number was their new phone number.

'Lolala, look at Mrs Stein's daughter. She married someone who is not Jewish. A nice man he seemed. An accountant. Look at her, Lolala. Three children, no money, dirty everything. He is in the pub every day straight after work, then he comes home and gives her a nice klup on the head. That's what will happen to you, Lolala, if you marry an Australian.'

Lola wasn't surprised at this prospect of violence. Lola knew that she didn't yet know half of how frightening the world was. She did know that there was danger everywhere, and that life was a series of narrow escapes. By the time she was thirteen she had a highly evolved, complex system of

warding off evil. She had to touch all the doorknobs and cupboard handles in her bedroom ten times each in the correct order, from left to right, before going to bed. Then she could sleep.

On Sunday nights the world looked better to Lola. In the afternoon Mrs Bensky would bake a sponge cake. It always came out with a soft brown covering, like lightly spun velvet. Next she laid out the bowls. A bowl of dark, shiny chocolates, a bowl of delicately sprigged branches of muscatel raisins scattered with almonds, a bowl of black, fat prunes, and a bowl of fruit-flavoured boiled lollies.

Then she prepared supper. It was always the same. Grated egg and spring onion salad, schmalz herring, smoked mackerel, chopped liver, dill pickles, radish flowers, sliced tomatoes, some rye bread and some matzoh. After that, she unfolded four card tables and chairs and arranged them in the small lounge room. At four o'clock Mr and Mrs Bensky had a nap for an hour. By eight o'clock the air was scented with heady perfume and cigarettes. Mrs Ganz's long, polished nails sparkled as she dealt the cards. Lola loved Mrs Ganz's husky voice and the way that her breasts moved with her breath.

Mr Ganz argued with Mr Berman: 'Chaim, you are an idiot! You walk with your eyes shut. You will be finished if you go into partnership with such an idiot like Felek Ganzgarten. You mustn't do it.'

'Gentlemen, gentlemen,' Mr Bensky admonished them in his most formal English.

Mrs Small sang in a low voice as she played. 'Motl, Motl vos vat sein mit dir, der Rabbi sogt du kanst nisht lernen,' she sang – 'Morris, Morris what is going to become of you, the Rabbi says you are not learning.'

And Mr Small, as usual, slipped Lola a couple of very expensive, large, chocolate-covered liqueur prunes. Mr Zelman whistled an old Polish lullaby as he smoothly swept his winnings over to his corner.

Sometimes the hum of the room was low and calm, and other times the atmosphere was feverish. Moves were disputed, news was dispensed, rumours were scotched or debated, advice was given and taken, and money was won and lost.

Mrs Bensky never played cards. She made cups of black lemon tea, refilled the glasses of soda water, emptied the ashtrays and served the supper.

Driving the children to school, Lola remembered Rodney, twenty-three years old, his speech almost a stutter that was expelled in short bursts. He had looked much happier when he was not speaking. And Lola was then free to imagine his thoughts.

One day, Rodney told her that he was never going to marry. He said that he would be too worried that his wife would leave him. This revelation was at odds with Lola's understanding of Rodney. She saw him as independent, self-contained and peaceful. The thought of not being the one who had to worry about being left appealed to Lola. Six weeks later they were married.

Lola and Rodney became good friends. They laughed together. They blossomed as parents and were bound together by a fierce pride in their two beautiful and clever children.

For the first few years of the marriage, Lola was captivated and wholly satisfied by Rodney's blondness. She would lie awake next to him for hours, looking at the golden hairs glinting on his arms.

Lola dropped the children off and parked the car in the supermarket car park. She walked to a taxi rank and caught a taxi to Garth's apartment.

In the taxi, the lies, the deception and the tension of the last month visited Lola briefly, but her happiness crept up and covered her.

Garth was waiting for her. His smile looked as though it might lift him off the ground. He trembled as he held her. He had prepared coffee. She watched him pour the coffee.

The first time they made love, Lola had felt like a virgin. She and Rodney had shuffled in and out of sex comfortably, companionably. Now she ached. She had forgotten what it was like to ache for a man. It felt like a violin screaming between her legs.

That evening at dinner, Rodney said 'I think Garth Walker is in love with you.'

'What?' she said.

'I've seen the way he looks at you,' Rodney answered. 'He doesn't take his eyes off you. He talks to the kids and he looks at you. He talks to me and he looks at you.'

'Don't be silly,' said Lola. She felt bilious.

'It's infatuation,' said Lola's closest friend, Margaret-Anne. 'It wears off. After a few years you and Garth will be like you and Rodney. It's not worth the bother.'

Lola fantasized about finding another wife for Rodney. She would find someone intelligent, well-read and with a good sense of humour, and they could all be friends. They could buy a small block of flats and create two large apartments. They could eat together. They could share holidays. And the children wouldn't miss out. The prospect of this happy communal life made Lola feel exhausted.

Lola knew it wasn't going to be easy to tell Mrs Bensky that she was going to leave Rodney.

'So, Hitler didn't kill me, now you are going to do it for him!' screamed Mrs Bensky.

Mr Bensky said: 'I lived through the labour camp to hear this news? I wish I would have died.'

Mrs Bensky rang Rodney to tell him that she would do his laundry. She said she didn't want Rodney to suffer the humiliation of having his clothes washed by a wife who was in love with someone else.

Lola had not had such an effect on her parents since the day she told them that she was going to marry Rodney.

'Lolala, Lolala, how can you do this to us?' Mrs Bensky had wailed. 'What will our friends say? They will say that we didn't bring you up properly. They will say that we should have sent you to Mount Scopus, not to an Australian school. Lola, get me some Stemetil. I feel sick.'

Now, Mr and Mrs Bensky were hysterical. 'Lola, you and Rodney were our big hope, our example of how a mixed marriage can work. Everyone says what a wonderful man Rodney is and what a wonderful couple you are. Lolala, wake up!' Mrs Bensky screamed.

For most of her adult life Lola had had trouble waking up. She used to daydream while she was cleaning, while she was driving, while she was reading or watching television, and while people spoke to her. She would nod from time to time, and on the whole no-one noticed.

She had a whole set of fantasies she could slip into. When Mrs Bensky delivered her regular lectures about losing weight, Lola would plug herself into the dream in which she had just completed her fifth best-selling novel. A novel that had made millions of readers weep. A novel that had earned Lola hundreds of thousands of dollars. A novel that had caused passionate debate in dining rooms in Paris, London and New York. Last week, when Mrs Bensky finished her speech, Lola was being interviewed by Johnny Carson on the *Tonight* show.

When she was with Garth, Lola was wide awake. So awake she could feel every part of her body. She could feel her nervous heart. She could feel her knees. She felt as though she could inhale the earth and touch the stars.

Garth taught her about art. He played her music. Mahler, Satie, Berg, Poulenc, Glass, Stravinsky. He read her poetry. Poems by Akhmatova, Tsvetayeva, Brodsky, William Carlos Williams. Poems by Anne Sexton. And he never stopped looking at her. He looked at her as they walked. He looked at her when they talked. He looked at her while they ate. He looked at her as they made love. And he painted her. He painted her happy and he painted her sad. He painted her pained and he painted her exuberant. He painted her as a madonna and he painted her as a warrior queen, a Boadicea streaking across the canvas. Hundreds of portraits of her were stacked around the walls of his studio.

Mr and Mrs Bensky had observed every detail of Lola's life. What she ate, how often she changed her underwear, who she spoke to in the school ground. Mrs Bensky would watch Lola every lunchtime, after she had delivered her daily hot lunch. Later on, Mrs Bensky kept a record of Lola's menstrual cycle on a chart inside the pantry cupboard. And the intercom system that connected all the rooms in the house was always switched on.

Everything was a potential catastrophe. A sneeze indicated pneumonia, a cough was a sign of asthma, a stomach ache pointed towards kidney and liver trouble. An unexpected knock at the door would leave Mrs Bensky breathless, and if Lola was ever late home from school, Mrs Bensky prepared herself for the worst.

Lola, who still complained that nothing she did escaped her parents' scrutiny, became an observant parent herself. Lola adored her son Julian. For the first year and a half of his life she recorded his every bowel movement. She drew up a chart and headed the columns 'Time', 'Size', 'Consistency' and 'Colour'. Another chart recorded every mouthful of food baby Julian swallowed. This was headed 'Food', 'Description', 'Amount', 'Time' and 'Attitude'.

By the time her daughter, Paradise, was born, Lola was not so intense about being a parent. She allowed Paradise to pat stray dogs and to eat her food from the kitchen floor. Paradise spent hours smudging her meals into the brown quarry tiles under the table before scraping the food into her mouth.

Lola worried about the consequences of allowing Paradise to eat off the floor, but she consoled herself with the thought that at least Paradise was a good eater. Julian was such a fussy eater that Lola had had to pretend that everything she fed him was chicken. Most of Julian's chicken chocolate custard or chicken fruit salad or chicken chops went into Lola.

Mr and Mrs Bensky spent the Saturday afternoons of most summers at St Kilda Beach. The whole gang would go. Mrs Bensky always brought cold boiled eggs and rye bread, and Mrs Ganz made her special carrot and pineapple salad. The Zelmans brought ham and Mr Pekelman brought long cucumbers from his garden.

They sat under the tea-trees on the foreshore, on thick, soft rugs, and ate and drank and talked. The Italian man who sold peanuts was always happy to see them. They bought twelve large bags. Enough peanuts to last until dinner.

Every now and then, someone would go for a dip in the water. Most of the gang couldn't swim. Mrs Bensky was the only good swimmer. She would stride into the water in her gold lamé bikini, or her silver and purple polka dotted pair, or the green pair covered in latex leaves.

As a child, Lola used to wear lumpy, frilly bathers. They had a gathered yoke and a full skirt, which Mrs Bensky said disguised Lola's hips and thighs.

Now, Lola would soon be able to wear her first pair of bikinis. The weight was dropping off her. Every day she was thinner. Garth satisfied all her appetites and she no longer felt hungry.

At five o'clock, Lola started getting ready to go home. Garth phoned for a taxi and then came and sat down next to her. 'Lola, I love you. I'll always love you. There'll never be anything in my life more important than loving you. I feel as though I was born to be with you.'

The next day, Lola told Rodney that she was moving out

with the children. All he said was 'Have you slept with him?'

'No,' she lied.

Garth, with his dark hair and large, heavy-lidded eyes, looked Jewish. Lola hoped that the Benskys would see this as progress.

You Will Be Going Back To Your Roots

Garth's new trousers had three pleats on either side of the zip. Until now he had worn skin-tight, peg-legged Levis. Lola looked at Garth. She found the loose space between his legs alluring. She started to think about what lay behind those parallel pleats.

Not since Lola was seventeen had she felt lustful just looking at a man's crotch.

Out of bed, Lola rarely felt sexually aroused. She had enough trouble feeling that way in bed. Where were the children? Could they hear? Was she ovulating? Should she use Ultrasure With Spermicidal Creme or Nuda Natural Feeling condoms? What was the time? Did she have to get up early in the morning? These were the questions that occupied Lola when sex seemed imminent.

A distant memory flickered in Lola's head. She quickly tried to calculate how old she would have been in the 1950s, when all men wore pleats in their pants. She had been just young enough still to sit on her father's lap and crush him with hugs when he came home from work.

Lola had always adored her father. She still did. She couldn't resist his generosity and his sense of humour. She loved the way that he turned beetroot red and cried when he laughed. If he laughed at the dinner table, pieces of fish or chicken would fly from his mouth and land on the other side of the kitchen.

Lola's girlfriends also adored her father. 'Mr Bensky, Mr Bensky, can you drive us to Luna Park?' they would beseech him. On Saturdays and Sundays Mr Bensky could be seen driving through the streets of Melbourne, his pink Pontiac Parisienne full of chattering, gum-chewing fourteen-year-olds.

If they passed Leo's Spaghetti Bar in Fitzroy Street, the girls knew that they could rely on Mr Bensky to shout them a round of chocolate gelatis.

Mr Bensky loved gelati. Before the war, in Lodz, Mr Bensky used to spend more money on ice-cream than most people earned in a week.

Mr Bensky came from one of the wealthiest Jewish families in Lodz. They owned apartment blocks and a timber yard. At sixteen, Mr Bensky was in charge of the timber yard. He doubled the turnover, fiddled the books and pocketed the profit. Nobody noticed.

Even as a schoolboy, Mr Bensky never used public transport. He went everywhere by droshky. He single-handedly supported two droshkies and their drivers. At eighteen he bought himself a dark red Skoda sports car.

Mr Bensky met Mrs Bensky when she was the very quiet, studious, extraordinarily beautiful Renia Kindler.

Mr and Mrs Kindler lived in two small rooms with their seven children. Mrs Kindler paid the caretaker of their block a couple of zlotys extra a week to keep one of the external toilets solely for the use of the Kindler family.

Renia's ambition was to study medicine. She was not easily deterred from her studies.

Mr Bensky wooed this slim-hipped, serious sixteen-year-old fervently. He bought her an eighteen-carat solid gold Rolex watch. He bought her French perfumes and Swiss chocolates. He bought her peaches and strawberries, and the first pineapple that she had ever seen.

Just as Renia was preparing to leave for the University of Vienna, Germany invaded Poland. All the Jews living in Lodz were ordered to move to a slum area of the city, where they were completely cut off from the rest of the world.

Mr and Mrs Kindler urged Renia to marry Mr Bensky. They thought that she would be better off with his family.

In their haste and confusion, the Benskys had only been able to pack a few valuables. At the end of that first year in the ghetto, they were as poor and as hungry as everyone else. They had sold their last diamond, a blue-white, 2.4-carat stone in a heavy eighteen-carat gold setting, for a sack of potato peels.

Potato peels were a luxury in the ghetto. You had to have good connections in the public kitchens to buy this deli-cacy. You also had to know whether the kitchens used knives to peel their potatoes. Peels from the kitchens that used potato peelers were mostly just films of dirt.

Lola hated hearing about the potato peels. It seemed too pathetic. Worse than the stories about children dying in the streets and relatives killing each other for a piece of bread and trainload after trainload of people being shipped out of the ghetto never to be heard of again.

When Lola was twelve, she had boiled herself a pot of potato peels. She had often wondered what they tasted like. She was halfway through her first mouthful when Mrs Bensky came home unexpectedly. Mrs Bensky, who had never laid a hand on either of her daughters, took the bowl of potato peels. Then, screaming and crying, she shook Lola by the hair until Lola fainted.

The thought of her father's penis made Lola feel nauseous. If she thought about her father in sexual terms, she would have to think about him fucking her mother. She tried to blink that thought out of her head.

At seventeen, Lola was having furtive sex regularly, if erratically, with her first serious boyfriend. One evening, with her puce-faced boyfriend hovering above her, Lola was suddenly seized with the thought that maybe her parents were doing the same thing in their bedroom across the hallway. Her stomach heaved, and she vomited and vomited.

Fortunately, Lola's boyfriend considered himself an existential eccentric. He felt that this messy, smelly, potentially humiliating episode merely added to the interesting experiences of his life.

Melbourne is a small city. Years later, people still asked Lola if it was true that she had chucked all over Johnny Rosenberg while he was fucking her.

Mrs Bensky rarely touched Lola or her sister. When she kissed them hello and goodbye, she planted the peck firmly in mid-air.

Every evening when Mr Bensky came home from work, he would grab Mrs Bensky by the bum, and kiss her loudly. Mrs Bensky would try to shrug him off. 'Look at your beautiful mummy,' he would say to the girls. 'My little Renia. What a beauty!' By this time, Mrs Bensky would have wriggled out of his grip and busied herself serving dinner.

'You'll be going back to your roots if you marry me' was one of the lines that Garth used to persuade Lola to leave her husband. He pursued her relentlessly. He phoned her several times a day, wrote poems for her, painted her portrait, bought her an eighteen-carat gold Parker pen and a leather-bound notebook. Then came the jewellery. Lola loved rings. Garth bought her garnet rings, emerald rings, ruby rings, sapphire rings and a magnificent art-deco diamond ring.

In the end, Lola couldn't resist the adoration. Even before her analysis, Lola knew that she loved being adored. And Garth adored her. He was always looking at her. In seven years he had painted over five hundred portraits of her. Last year he had had an exhibition of his paintings in Sydney. The exhibition was called *Pictures of Lola*. One hundred and eight portraits of Lola hung from the walls of the Creighton Galleries.

Lola got up from the breakfast table. 'I think I'll have a shower,' she said to Garth.

Lola found it difficult to wash. She found it an ordeal. Lola only showered when she had to wash her hair.

Mrs Bensky showered every morning and every evening. And at night, if Mr and Mrs Bensky had made love. Lola used to hear the bathroom taps gushing at full throttle while Mrs Bensky furiously washed herself out.

Mrs Bensky kept her house as clean as she kept her body. She washed the floors every day. Twice a week she stripped the stove and the fridge. Once a week, balancing a large bucket of water on top of a ladder, she cleaned the windows. Mrs Bensky vacuumed the carpet when Mr Bensky and the girls left in the mornings, and again after dinner.

Sometimes Lola didn't change her pantihose for a fortnight. The feet would become rigid. Lola wondered if the dirt held the pantihose together and made them last longer.

Mr and Mrs Bensky visited Lola every Tuesday and Friday night. They usually stayed for about three-quarters of an hour.

For years Lola felt that they only came to see the children. They were besotted by their grandchildren. Mr Bensky would look at Lola's son, Julian, who at sixteen was already six feet tall, and say 'Whoever would have thought I would live to have grandchildren?'

Mrs Bensky would go straight to Lola's kitchen sink, in her Yves St Laurent silk blouse, her Kenzo trousers and her Maud Frizon shoes, and wash and scour and dry until everything gleamed.

Even at home, Mrs Bensky never wore an apron or work clothes. She cleaned in her ordinary clothes, although Mrs Bensky's clothes could hardly be described as ordinary. She had satin dresses beaded with pearls, taffeta coats dripping diamantés, lamé and lurex cocktail dresses, linen and leather trousers, all from the best fashion houses in Europe.

Margaret-Anne and Ivana, Lola's best friends, kept spotless houses. Ivana felt compelled to clean up whenever she visited Lola. Margaret-Anne said that she found Lola's mess relaxing.

Margaret-Anne and Ivana were both tall and thin. Mrs Bensky was very slim too. Lola wondered whether ectomorphs had a mania for cleanliness.

Lola never used to wash the dishes. She owned enough crockery to keep going between the cleaning woman's twice-weekly visits. After her first year in analysis, Lola began to wash her own dishes. Late in life, Lola discovered the joy of well-scrubbed saucepans and shiny surfaces.

Lola had always had trouble with the concept of moderation. For a while she became a bit obsessive. She washed every teaspoon or fork or coffee mug as soon as it was used. She cleaned out the pantry and bathroom cupboards and put everything in labelled jars. She rearranged the cutlery drawers and the crockery cabinets. She vacuumed the front veranda and polished the letterbox. She drove everyone crazy, and the kids begged her to go back to being a slob.

Garth stood next to Lola. He wound his leg around her leg and stroked her face. The children were at school. They lay down and had a noisy fuck.

After she came, Lola wept and wept. She often cried after a strong orgasm. She knew that it usually meant that she had been shutting herself off from any intense emotions, been out of touch with her sadness.

Lola used to say that she felt that she was born with a backlog of sadness. She didn't really know what she meant. Was it all those dead relatives – uncles, aunts, cousins, grandmothers and grandfathers – all fed to the sky? The ashes of the victims of Auschwitz almost choked the Vistula river.

Mr and Mrs Bensky shared a past that Lola could never belong to. Lola longed to drive a wedge into their togetherness. She had one such moment of triumph when she was ten. She had been begging and pleading to have her ears pierced. Mrs Bensky said that ear-piercing was a barbaric custom and they were a civilized family. Not while Lola lived in her house could she have pierced ears.

Lola stopped practising the piano. She no longer took the dog for a walk. She sat in her room for hours looking miserable. Mr Bensky relented. Behind Mrs Bensky's back, he took Lola into the city and held her hand while a nursing sister pierced Lola's ears.

For the next week, Mrs Bensky made twice as much noise as she washed up while the rest of the family ate their dinner.

Lola still wore the gold sleeper earrings that Mr Bensky had bought. Now a gold, heart-shaped Victorian locket carrying a lock of Garth's hair hung from the sleeper in Lola's right ear.

'Lola, my love, my beautiful wife, my delicious chicken, shall we go out for coffee?' Garth called from the bedroom.

'OK, I'll be out of the shower in a second,' she answered.

Lola loved going out for coffee. Going out for a coffee meant going out for a walk, going out for a cake, going out for a talk. She had seen some new earrings up the street. They were small ruby studs. Maybe she would have another look at them.

Chopin's Piano

Lola Bensky was about to arrive in Warsaw. She tried to decide whether she was nervous or anxious. Nervous was all right. Being anxious made her dizzy. She wondered if she should take a Valium. She didn't want to take a Valium if what she was feeling was a normal kind of tension. If it was anxiety, she needed the Valium.

The plane landed. An indecipherable blast of blurred Polish came from the loudspeaker system. Lola began to feel breathless. She hated not being able to understand or to make herself understood. In the bleak immigration and customs hall, long queues of people stood waiting. Lola was dismayed. She always tried to avoid standing in queues. It was one of the things that made her very anxious. Her analyst had explained to her that she felt this anxiety because she could not bear to have to wait for the breast. That she was angry about the fact that she was dependent on her mother. That she was outraged that her mother had something that she didn't. That she was jealous and envious of her mother, but couldn't face the pain of these bad feelings, and so denied her need for her mother. This insight hadn't helped Lola with her queue problem.

The yellow-haired, sallow-faced young man behind the immigration desk tapped his blue biro violently as he asked Lola questions.

'Your nationality?' he snapped.

Lola tried not to panic. He was holding her passport. Why would he ask her her nationality?

'Australian,' she said meekly.

'Purpose of visit?' he barked.

'To see Poland,' Lola whispered. She could see that he thought that this was a reasonable answer. With a brusque gesture, he motioned her to move on.

Outside it was dark and bitterly cold. Lola was flushed and hot. She could feel drops of sweat trickling down between her breasts. She was wearing a woollen spencer and long woollen underpants, a three-piece woollen suit, angora socks, boots, an astrakhan hat, elbow-length gloves and a voluminous, thick coat. A cashmere scarf was wound around her neck. She caught a taxi to the Victoria Hotel. Driving in, she was astonished to see that Warsaw looked like an ordinary city. The streets were lined with graceful neoclassical four and five-storey apartment buildings. A soft, yellow light that suggested happy family life seeped out from the sides of the curtained windows. There was no sign of menace in the air.

The Victoria Hotel was a 1960s late-modern building. Lola recognized the style. Caulfield was full of fine examples of this sort of building.

Lola was unnerved when she walked inside the hotel. The interior was a large replica of the loungerooms of Caulfield and Bellevue Hill. The same granite and marble surfaces, the same rich, rounded woodwork, the same heavy raw silk drapes, the same large leather lounge suites, and the same 1950s expressionist ashtrays and vases. Chandeliers hung from the ceiling.

The short, stocky woman who was to be her guide was waiting in the foyer. Lola explained to Mrs Potoki-Okolska that she had come to Poland to see her parents' past, the small piece of their past that was left.

She wanted to go to Lodz, she told Mrs Potoki-Okolska, to see where her parents had lived before the war. Where they had studied, where they had played, where they had walked. She would also like to see what was left of the Lodz ghetto. She explained that her parents had spent four and a half years in the Lodz ghetto before they were shipped to Auschwitz.

'My mother was the sole survivor of her family. Her brothers Shimek, Abramek, Jacob and Felek, and her sisters Fela, Bluma and Marilla, and her mother and father were gassed and then burnt. My father lost his parents, three brothers and a sister.'

'It was a terrible, terrible tragedy, yes,' said Mrs Potoki-Okolska. 'But Polish people lost people too. It was not just the Jews who were killed by the Nazis. We suffered. Oh, how we suffered! My mother's cousin lost her mother, an innocent woman who never hurt anybody.' Here, Mrs Potoki-Okolska had to pause. Tears were streaming down her face.

Mrs Potoki-Okolska showed Lola to her hotel room. A sign on the back of the door asked that no guests remain in the room after 10 p.m. Lola assumed that that meant guests other than those who were paying.

The fridge in the room was full of bottles of blackcurrant juice, blackcurrant juice with vodka, and Coca-Cola. Mrs Potoki-Okolska drank four bottles of Coca-Cola. She thanked Lola profusely for the Coca-Cola, said goodnight and left.

Lola looked out of the window. Warsaw was asleep. The city was covered in a fine layer of snow. Everything looked peaceful.

'It will be the end of you. They will put you in jail,' Mrs Bensky had warned Lola. 'They won't let you leave Poland. The Poles were worse than the Germans. They used to laugh at us in our concentration-camp rags. Small children would kick us when we were walking to work in the towns near the camp. Oh, those nice Poles, those good people, they couldn't wait to point Jews out to the Germans. They couldn't wait to take over our apartments when we had to move to the ghetto. They took our clothes, our china, our furniture. They took over the Jewish businesses. They just helped themselves. The caretaker of my parents' building, who my mother had looked after like she was one of the family, went running to the Gestapo to report on us.

'And after the war, there was a miracle. Not one single Polish person did know anything about what happened to us. You could smell the flesh burning for kilometres from Auschwitz. Those chimneys were blowing smoke twenty-four hours a day. The sky was red day and night, but the Poles didn't notice.

'And when my cousin Adek went back after the war, what did he see? He saw that they were surprised that he was still alive. Mrs Boleswaf, the caretaker, said to him: "Oh, I thought all of you were dead." Her son was wearing my father's suit, Adek said. My brother's grand piano was in the middle of their living room. And Mrs Boleswaf offered him a cup of tea from the beautiful white-and-silver china that was part of my mother's dowry. What do you want to go to Poland for? Something terrible will happen to you.'

In the morning light, the city looked less vibrant. Lola was shocked at how depressed and oppressed the people looked. They walked with their heads down. Even the children were quiet and expressionless. Men and women wore grey clothes and grey faces. Their hair was lank and dull. No shampoo, Lola remembered.

Long queues of people waited outside the sparsely stocked shops. There was no movement in the queues. No-one spoke. Lola found this collective depression frightening. She had always thought of depression as an individual and isolating experience.

At the bus stop, people stood in silence. The bus arrived. The crowd clambered aboard, elbowing each other and Lola out of the way. Lola was left behind. From the bus,

Mrs Potoki-Okolska screamed at Lola that she would get off at the next stop and walk back.

By midday Lola had seen the Radziwill palace, the Potoki palace, the Tyszkiewicz palace, the Uruski palace, the Czapski palace, the Staszic palace, a dozen churches and several cathedrals. Mrs Potoki-Okolska left money in each church, and wept as she dedicated the gift to her mother. In the Church of St Cross there was an urn that contained Chopin's heart. The Old Town Market Square, like most of the city of Warsaw, had been destroyed by the Nazis. Mrs Potoki-Okolska pointed to one quaint seventeenth-century building after another and announced: 'Built in 1953,' or 'Built in 1956,' or 'This building is still being finished.'

Lola was exhausted. Her feet hurt. She was suffering from the anxiety that she experienced when she was ignored. Mrs Potoki-Okolska had refused to listen to her when she had expressed her lack of interest in churches, palaces or monuments to famous generals.

Lola had arranged to have lunch with Mr Konrad Serbin, the father of a friend of a friend. She felt that it could do her no harm to have a connection with Mr Serbin, who was one of Poland's leading barristers, and his wife, a highly acclaimed surgeon.

Lola wanted to buy some flowers for Mrs Serbin. Mrs Potoki-Okolska took Lola to a small, dimly lit, shabby shop. The back wall of the shop was lined with shelves. Each shelf held three vases, and each vase contained two flowers. A carnation and a freesia. A round, red-faced man was meticulously wrapping a pink carnation in a small square of butcher's paper.

Lola asked Mrs Potoki-Okolska to ask for a dozen carnations. Mrs Potoki-Okolska looked horrified.

'It is very rude to buy so many flowers,' she said. 'Your friend's father will think that you want to show him how much money you have. It is not good manners, no, not good manners.'

Mrs Potoki-Okolska was very concerned with good manners. This morning at breakfast she had wrenched a tooth-pick from Lola's hands. 'This is not good manners in Poland,' she had shouted.

The carnations were thin and stringy. Lola thought that twelve of them would at least produce some volume.

'What to do? What to do? What to do?' sighed Mrs Potoki-Okolska.

Mrs Potoki-Okolska ordered a dozen carnations. A rumble of hostility went through the waiting queue. The florist glared at Lola and wrapped the carnations carelessly. Twelve carnations cost as much as most people earned in a week. Flower-growers were the new rich in Poland.

Mrs Potoki-Okolska was right. Mrs Serbin looked furious when Lola gave her the flowers.

Mr and Mrs Serbin were wealthy Poles. Their two-room apartment was filled with nineteenth-century romantic and historical paintings, oriental rugs, leather-bound books, silver and crystal.

The Serbins were very pleased with the parcel of pencils, biros, soaps, toothpaste, pantihose, silver foil and kitchen cloths that Lola had brought from their daughter. Mr Serbin's brother and sister-in-law joined them for lunch. Mrs Serbin served an entrée of smoked trout with horse-radish sauce. In the middle of a mouthful of trout, it occurred to Lola that all five Poles at the table were in their mid-sixties. The same age as Mr and Mrs Bensky. Where were they when the Jews were being rounded up for the ghetto? Where were they when the Warsaw ghetto was burning? Were they part of the heated, cheering crowd on the Aryan side? Were they watching Jews explode into the night?

Lola felt nauseous. She excused herself, and ran to the toilet. The toilet was in a tiny room, ten feet away from the dining table. The door wouldn't close properly. Lola tried to hold the door shut with her foot while she sat on the toilet. She felt bilious and giddy. Sweat ran down her face.

She could hear every word of the lunch-table conversation. She coughed loudly to disguise her own violent eruptions. Half an hour later, she emerged. Mrs Potoki-Okolska rushed to greet her. 'You look terrible. Was it your liver or your kidneys?' she asked.

Mrs Serbin brought in a large jar of Nescafé on an enormous Georgian silver platter. She put six spoonfuls of the coffee powder into each person's cup. Lola asked if she could have tea. The other guests drank their coffee with relish.

The next morning Lola met Mrs Potoki-Okolska at the railway station at eight-thirty. At eleven o'clock there was an announcement that the nine o'clock train to Lodz had been cancelled. Mrs Potoki-Okolska rushed Lola to the taxi stand.

Lola looked at the miserable faces in the taxi queue. She felt buoyed by their hardship.

'You've got what you deserve,' she whispered to the man standing on her left.

Lola sat in the back of the taxi. Mrs Potoki-Okolska sat in the front seat. She ordered the taxi driver to turn the heater on high, and settled down with a bag of boiled sweets.

Lola had packed her own provisions. She had packets of Life Savers, Minties and Steam Rollers. Steam Rollers, Lola felt, were particularly good for combating nausea.

After an hour in the car Lola felt sick. Her skin burned and itched. She unbuttoned her coat and jacket. Her chest was covered with angry red blotches. She thought that she was probably the only person in Poland suffering from a heat rash.

She opened the car window a little.

'What is that?' bellowed Mrs Potoki-Okolska. 'Shut it, shut it, shut it. You will catch a disease of the lungs. It is very dangerous. Very, very dangerous.' Lola closed the window.

They arrived at Zelazowa-Wola, Chopin's birthplace. Lola was glad to be able to get out of the car. An hour and a half later, Lola had seen Chopin's piano, Chopin's mother's piano, Chopin's bedroom, Chopin's mother's bedroom, Chopin's garden and Chopin's bathroom.

Lola thought that maybe she would never get to Lodz. She thought, once again, that maybe Lodz didn't exist. Maybe Mr and Mrs Bensky's past would always be inaccessible to her. Mrs Potoki-Okolska left Zelazowa-Wola reluctantly, humming *La Polonaise*.

They passed kilometre after kilometre of flat, snow-covered countryside. This soft, white stillness was punctuated occasionally by small forests of spindly, black fir trees.

They were now ten kilometres from Lodz. Lola was already weeping.

Friday Is A Good Day For Fish

Lola lay facing away from Garth. She was almost asleep. Garth had been rubbing her shoulders. He had patted her and rubbed her and stroked her. She felt suspended in a state of bliss.

Garth lowered his head and kissed her in a line across her back. He pressed himself against her. His rubbing became more intense. He was no longer soothing her into sleep. He was waking her.

Lola, at forty, could still sometimes feel nervous and shy about sex. She turned towards Garth. She buried her head in his chest. She loved his smell. They hadn't made love for over a week. She stroked him and smoothed him. She stroked his penis. She rocked it from side to side between her thumb and her forefinger. She felt good.

'My mother really loved the dress we bought her,' she said. 'I'm glad I didn't buy a book or that kettle. I felt so happy seeing my mother's pleasure.'

Garth started laughing. 'You're playing with me in the same absent-minded way you twist your hair. My dick is flying backwards and forwards and you're talking about your mother's birthday present.'

Garth pulled her on top of him.

'Can we change positions before we come? Can you lie on top of me then?' she said.

He laughed. 'Do you have to orchestrate everything? Do you have any more instructions?'

They made love. Lola gripped the sheet. She used it to lever herself. 'It's OK,' she said. 'We don't have to change positions.'

Lola had a long orgasm. She felt as though she'd been away. In another dimension. In another time. She fell asleep.

Lola was in Lodz. She was in the loungeroom of the apartment. Everything was exactly as her father had described it. The rounded couch and chairs, the white-tiled heater. All that was missing was the family. Her father's parents, his three brothers and sister.

They had known the end was coming. Jengelef Boleswaf, the family's Polish caretaker, who was eighty-three when Lola visited him in Poland, had told Lola this.

'Your grandfather came to me before he left for the ghetto. He said to me, "I may not be here in a few years time, but my building will still be here in one hundred years,"' Jengelef had said.

Nobody had ever said 'your grandfather' to Lola.

Jengelef still lived on the ground floor of the apartments that Lola's grandfather had built. Jengelef lived in one small room. Everything in the room was spotless. A small table next to the window was covered with a starched white linen tablecloth. The corners of the tablecloth were embroidered with red roses. In the middle of the room was a plain brass bed.

Jengelef's wife was lying in the bed. She was dying. She was lying perfectly still. She seemed to be barely breathing. Her skin was pale and clear, and her hair was brushed and fluffed. She was wearing a white pin-tucked nightie. Jengelef's devotion to his wife had made Lola cry. But then, Lola had cried all the time that she was in Lodz.

When Lola had arrived in Lodz, she had gone straight to 23 Zakatna Street. The taxi driver had pulled up across the

road from the apartments. From the car window she could
see the first-floor balcony her father had told her about so
many times. His father used to sit on the balcony and watch
his children come home from school. Lola's father always
made sure that he had his school cap on before he came into
his father's line of vision.

Lola got out of the taxi and stood on the footpath. She
was too frightened to cross the empty street. Her heart was
pounding and she was trembling. She crossed the street.
The main entrance of the building was open. Lola stepped
inside.

She stood in the deserted hallway. Her chest tightened
and her throat constricted. She found it hard to breathe.
She stood in the deserted hallway. The air felt thick with
people. She could feel their presence. She could hear their
voices. The voices of people going about their daily business. Going to work, to school, to market. She could feel
the movement. She could feel the life. She stood in the
hallway and wept and wept.

Lola cried every time she went to the building. She went
there every day. Often she stood in the hallway for hours.
She would touch the tiled wall with her cheek. She would
stroke the balustrade. She wanted to sink into the marble
staircase. To mesh herself with the air. To be part of the
past.

Jengelef had told the tenants in the building who Lola
was. Some of them had looked at Lola as though she was a
ghost. 'I thought they had killed all the Jews from Lodz,'
Mr Krupnik from the second floor had said to Lola.

Lola was washing her hair when the phone rang. She had
never been able to ignore a ringing telephone. She answered
the phone. Shampoo dripped down her.

'It's me, Morris,' said Lola's friend, Morris Lubofsky.

'Hi, Morris,' said Lola. Morris sounded a bit flat.

'What's wrong?' she asked.

'I've just found out my brother is coming to Melbourne

for two months,' said Morris. 'My folks are putting pressure on me to invite him to stay at my place. I'm not happy about having him back in the country, let alone in my house.'

Morris and his brother Boris were twins. Fraternal, not identical twins. Boris, a banker, had lived in New York since he was twenty. Lola thought that Boris was OK. She couldn't see that Morris had all that much to complain about in Boris. He hardly saw him.

'Maybe you and Boris will patch things up this visit? We're a bit old to be quibbling with our siblings,' said Lola. Quibbling with our siblings. Lola liked the sound of that line. Quibbling with our siblings. She repeated it to herself a few times while Morris complained about Boris.

Morris was calling from Sydney. He'd been there for a week. 'Sydney's depressing me,' he said. 'Everybody looks slightly seedy. On the make. I must be getting old. And the drug scene here is depressing. Everyone's on cocaine or Ecstasy. Really, fifty per cent of my friends are on cocaine.'

Lola thought that she and Morris were both getting old. This was the same Morris Lubofsky who used to slip her joints and speed and phials of LSD when they were twenty. These drugs, Morris used to tell her, would expand her mind and her horizons. Lola was having enough trouble with her mind at the time. Her grip on things already seemed marginal and skewwhiff, and Lola didn't want it tilted any further. The contortions that LSD produced were too chaotic for Lola. As a fellow seeker of purity, enlightenment and truth, Lola had been a great disappointment to Morris.

Lola had pulled on a dressing gown while Morris was talking. Her hair was still dripping. She felt uncomfortable. She felt fat this morning. She'd eaten too much poppy-seed cake last night. Lola allowed herself a slice of poppy-seed cake every Thursday. Last night's slice had been just short of half the cake.

'Yeah, fifty per cent of my friends have got a coke

problem,' said Morris.

'Fifty per cent of my friends have got a cake problem, Morris,' said Lola. 'I better go,' she said. 'I was in the shower when you rang and I've probably already caught pneumonia.'

'See you in Melbourne next week,' said Morris.

Lola hopped back into the shower. She rinsed out the shampoo, towel-dried and moussed her hair, and got dressed. She looked around. Her two desks were clear. Her poems were filed. Her pencils were sharpened. Everything was ready for her to begin work.

Lola looked at the poem that she was currently struggling with. What was she trying to say? She was trying to say that she was getting better. That she was changing. That she could see that she could no longer occupy the role of the victim.

Spotting the fault had been her speciality. Lola always knew whose fault it was. It was always someone else's. She was also an expert on what was wrong. Lola could find the flaw in anything. You could tell Lola the most elevating news, and in less than ten seconds she could tell you what was worrying about it.

Just before lunchtime, Lola's mother rang. 'Lola darling, Genia Pekelman is giving me a lift to the Georges sale. They have got a sale of all their imported underwear. Darling, would you like to come with us?' said Renia.

'I don't think so, Mum,' said Lola. 'I've got such a lot to do.'

'They have got silk petticoats and beautiful strapless bras and backless bras and Swiss cotton underpants. Lola darling, they have got Lily of France bras,' said Renia.

Renia always wore beautiful underwear. She had drawers and drawers of bras and girdles and suspender belts and petticoats.

For years, Lola had refused to wear any underwear. Then she went through a phase of wearing ragged and discoloured underwear. She would wear torn and stained underwear underneath beautifully beaded and embroidered dresses.

'We won't be long in the city, darling,' said Renia. 'Genia doesn't feel so good today, so we will just go straight in and straight home. I just want to buy some bras and Genia just wants to buy some underpants.'

Lola was beginning to get a headache. She didn't want to go shopping for underpants with Genia Pekelman.

When Lola was thirteen, Genia Pekelman had told her a story that had horrified her. 'When I was your age,' Genia had said to Lola, 'the Germans invaded Poland. I was walking down the street, and a whole car of German soldiers stopped me. They made me take off my underpants and clean the windscreen of their car with my underpants. All five of them stood outside the car while I was cleaning. One of them kept lifting my skirt so everyone in the street could see.'

'Mum, I really don't think I can come with you,' said Lola. 'Maybe you could buy me a white Lily of France bra in size 14C, and a black half-slip in a 16?'

'You don't need a 16,' said Renia. 'You've lost so much weight.'

'Yes I do,' said Lola. 'My hips are enormous.'

'No, you have lost enough weight. You don't need to lose any more. You look very nice. You shouldn't be too thin,' said Renia.

Lola was still not used to this turn of events. After being harangued all her life to lose weight, she now had to worry about being too thin. Too thin. If only she was too thin. If she was too thin she could have some more poppy-seed cake.

'Lola darling, give Lina a ring,' said Renia. 'She is your sister. Sisters should be sisters. And after all, you are the older one.' Lola wondered how old she would have to be before she was no longer considered the older one.

Last week Renia and Josl had had a large dinner party to

celebrate their forty-seventh wedding anniversary. Everyone was eating and talking except for Lina. Lina was picking at a plate of lettuce and cucumber.

Lina asked Renia if there were any chicken bones.

'Yes, of course, darling,' said Renia. She brought out a platter of chicken bones. Lina picked up a thigh bone and chewed it. Lola leaned across the table.

'If you're on a diet you shouldn't be chewing chicken bones,' she said.

'Chicken bones can't have any calories,' said Lina.

'Well, they do,' said Lola. 'The marrow is very fatty, and there's fat wedged in behind the gristle.' Lina put the bone down and returned to her lettuce.

'Are chicken bones really calorific?' Garth asked later.

'I don't know,' said Lola.

'Oy, darling, I have to go,' said Renia. 'Genia and Izak are here to pick me up. Bye bye, darling.'

So, Izak Pekelman was taking the women shopping. Jewish men were amazing, thought Lola. They did everything for their wives. They shopped, chauffeured, accompanied. Even on underwear excursions.

Lola liked Izak Pekelman. He always seemed to be in good spirits. Izak was respected and admired by all of his friends for his gardening skills. Not too many Jews were good in the garden. In his garden in Caulfield, Izak had almond trees, walnut trees, chestnut trees, apricot, pear, peach and plum trees, and orange, lemon and lime trees. Izak grew his own vegetables, too. He grew zucchinis, cauliflowers, cabbage, carrots, beans, peas, potatoes and spring onions.

When he was a child in Lowicz, Izak was in charge of the family's vegetable plot. He grew carrots, beetroots, onions, potatoes and radishes. Before and after school, every day, Izak had looked after his vegetables.

In the ghetto, where people were dying of starvation every day, Izak kept his mother and father alive with his vegetables. Izak grew onions and radishes and potatoes in an old pram. He had bought the pram from his cousin for a loaf of bread and his mother's wedding ring. Izak had kept the pram by his side all the time. He slept with the pram next to his mattress, and during the day, while he worked, he parked the pram outside the window where he sat sewing uniforms for the Germans.

'People did laugh at me,' he had told Lola. 'If there was some sunshine I would rush outside to move the pram. I had a chain to lock the wheels of the pram, and some wires over the vegetables so no-one could steal them quickly. One day I was at the pictures in Melbourne when a man came up to me and said: "You are the boy who grew vegetables in that old pram. My mother used to say to me that you looked after those vegetables like they were the most precious children in the world." To tell you the truth, Lola, I started to cry in the middle of the picture theatre when he was talking about my pram.'

Izak Pekelman always wore sandals. Sandals and socks. He wore sandals and socks in summer and in winter. To the beach and to barmitzvahs. When he was poor he was laughed at, in his socks and sandals. Now that he was wealthy, business associates admired his eccentricity.

Izak couldn't wear shoes. His toes were twisted and bent. His toenails were black, layered and chalky. They sat, raised and rounded, on top of his toes.

Lola had once asked Izak Pekelman why he always wore sandals. 'My feet don't look so nice,' he had said.

'What's wrong with them?' Lola had asked. For a moment Izak had looked as though he wasn't going to answer Lola's question, and then he spoke.

'In the concentration camp, Sachsenhausen, where I was in,' he said, 'they had an area for testing shoes. One of the local manufacturers wanted to test their merchandise on a variety of surfaces. So they did some research, and they built tracks with nine different surfaces. Every day some of us prisoners had to put on new shoes and walk for about forty kilometres over tracks of different sorts of cement, cinders, broken stones, sand, gravel. To make life more interesting for themselves, the SS guards made us wear shoes that were one or two sizes too small, and we had to carry sacks filled with twenty kilos of sand. So you can see, Lola, that I am lucky that I have still got toes.'

Lola couldn't speak. She felt terrible for asking Izak about his sandals. Izak didn't look upset. He looked calm.

'I always knew I was a lucky man,' he said. 'I was lucky even when I arrived in Sachsenhausen. When we got off the train there was a big crowd of people to greet us at the station. The spectacle of watching the prisoners arrive was an exciting pastime for the townspeople of Oranienburg. There were men and women and mothers with their children all watching us. When we got off the train they sang and shouted and screamed terrible things about the Jews, and they threw stones at us, and pieces of wood, and dirt from the street. We had to walk two miles from the station to the concentration camp, and the SS guards kicked us and beat us all the way. If somebody fell, they shot him. We had a whole trail of dead and injured. A few patrol cars drove along the road behind us to pick up the victims. It didn't matter whether they were dead or alive, they were all picked up because the SS had to deliver the correct total number of prisoners that had been consigned to the camp. This was German efficiency.

'One of the first things I saw when I arrived in Sachsenhausen was a sign which said: "There is a road to freedom. Its milestones are obedience, industry, honesty, order, cleanliness, sobriety, truthfulness, spirit of sacrifice and love for the Fatherland."

'I was lucky to see this sign. My friend Felix had died in the train that brought us to Sachsenhausen, and my cousin Moishe was beaten when he got off the train, and was shot when he fell down.'

At four o'clock, Lola decided to pack her work away for the day. The poem was working well, and she felt happy. She decided to prepare dinner early; she liked the feeling of being ahead of schedule. Maybe tonight she would make a nice potato and onion soup, and a light pasta.

Lola was chopping up her fourth large onion when the front door bell rang. It was Renia and Genia and Izak.

'Hello, hello, hello,' they chorused. Genia and Renia looked flushed and elated. The shopping had obviously been a success.

Renia looked beautiful. Her skin was golden and smooth. She was wearing a double-breasted, black Chanel suit. She looked stunning. Renia had looked much happier lately, thought Lola. It had happened slowly, over the last few years. Her happiness suited her, thought Lola.

'It was a very good sale, darling,' said Renia. 'I bought you six Lily of France bras, and three petticoats. Genia bought herself the most beautiful Swiss cotton underpants with a matching camisole singlet, and I did buy myself Christian Dior silk stockings for a quarter of their normal price.'

'We also went to Myers,' said Renia. 'I bought you a challah, some brisket and some gefilte fish. Everything from Myers. You can buy a very good challah in Myers. The fish is very good too. Friday is a very good day for fish. It is always fresh on Friday.'

Izak took Lola aside. He had a new joke. He knew Renia didn't approve of his jokes.

'Did you hear about Mrs Rosenberg?' Izak asked Lola. 'The phone rang in Mrs Rosenberg's flat. She answered the phone. "Hello," she said. It was a man on the phone. "I know what you want," he says. "You want me to come over and tear your clothes off. You want me to shtoop you stupid. You want me to tie you to the bed and shtoop you silly," he says. "From one hello you can tell all this?" said Mrs Rosenberg.'

Lola laughed.

'We should leave now, otherwise we will catch all the traffic,' said Renia. 'Goodbye, darling, enjoy the fish.'

Lola kissed Renia, Genia and Izak goodbye. 'Goodbye, goodbye, goodbye,' they called.

Five minutes later the trio were back.

'I forgot to give you the horseradish to eat with the fish. Garth loves this horseradish,' said Renia.

'Thanks, Mum. Goodbye,' said Lola.

'Goodbye, goodbye,' called Genia and Izak. Lola didn't know whether to laugh or cry. She could see the goodness, the kindness and the love in this frenzy, this intensity. So why did it still give her a headache? Maybe after another couple of years of analysis she would know the answer.

Lola and Garth ate alone that night. The children were in Sydney visiting Garth's parents.

'This is fabulous gefilte fish,' said Garth.

'It's from Myers,' said Lola. 'My mother has always said that the gefilte fish in Myers is very good. She's said so many things that I haven't listened to. I wonder what else I've missed out on.'

After dinner, Lola and Garth went to the opening of Stephen Newsome's exhibition of paintings at the Smithson Galleries. Newsome was an old friend of Garth's.

Lola disliked openings. The harsh lighting in galleries often heightened her anxiety. Standing up and talking to people also made her anxious. Tonight she would made an effort not to focus on herself. She wouldn't examine herself minutely for symptoms of anxiety. She wouldn't concentrate all her energy on the question of whether she was feeling anxious. She wondered if other people had to make such a conscious effort not to think about themselves all the time.

Lola and Garth told Stephen Newsome how much they liked his paintings, but Newsome was so drunk he could hardly recognize them. He was so drunk he could hardly stand.

'Newsome and I have both, over the years, had a lot of trouble standing up,' Lola said to Garth. 'He's been pissed, and I've been dizzy.' Lola and Garth said hello and goodbye to half a dozen people, and left the gallery.

At home, Lola prepared herself for bed. She cleansed and scrubbed and creamed her face. She looked at herself in the mirror. She looked so Jewish. Jewish eyes, Jewish curls, Jewish expression. She had a Jewish face. A face that looked semi-anxious when she was happy, and distressed when she was sad.

Lola turned her face away from the mirror. If she was going to work at making this analysis successful she would have to place less emphasis on what she looked like. She used to think that if her curls were at the right angle, everything else would be all right.

Lola walked out of the bathroom, through the lounge-room and into Garth's studio. Garth was painting. Luciano Pavarotti was singing 'Nessun dorma'. Garth's hips and legs moved in time to the music. He was immersed in his canvas, and didn't hear her come in.

She stood and watched him. She thought about how lucky she was. She was lucky to have Garth. Lucky to have the children. She was lucky. The thought took her by surprise. She felt temporarily disconcerted. It wasn't an aberrant thought, just a new one.

She kissed Garth goodnight. Still feeling lucky, Lola walked back to the bedroom. She knew that Garth was going to paint until late, so she had made herself a hot-water bottle. She got into bed. The new sheets she had bought felt nice. She hugged the hot-water bottle. Still feeling lucky, she fell asleep.

I Heard You Got Another Husband

For ten years Lola had not been able to mix with Jews. For ten years, even to walk along Acland Street, past the Scheherezade Restaurant, past the Benedykt Brothers Delicatessen, caused Lola anxiety.

She knew most of the people who stood in small clusters on the footpath, talking. 'Lolala, hello, what's happened to you? Last time I saw you, you were thin, now look.' Lola didn't have to say much in these encounters. 'Good morning, Lola, I heard you got divorced and now I heard you got another husband.'

Garth loved Acland Street. He always greeted Tivele, who had Parkinson's disease and shook dangerously as he drank his lemon tea, with a pat on the back and a handshake. He asked Abe how the hosiery business was going. He smiled like a benign parent while Adek, Edek and Isaac talked. They talked and talked. Over the top of each other. At the same time. What energy they had, this gang of elderly men! thought Lola. Everything mattered. Everything was important.

Lola went into the Scheherezade. She sat at a table near the counter. She ordered a glass of borscht and a plate of boiled potatoes. She watched Mr Krongold, who was at the back of the restaurant, eating his latkes in his parka and his peaked cap. He had already had schnitzel and boiled potatoes. Mr Krongold was a slightly built, fine-boned man. He ate vigorously.

Lola often ate bent over the rubbish bin. She tore clumps of bread from a loaf. One piece of bread into her mouth, one piece into the bin, some more for her, and a few crusty pieces for the rubbish bin. Lola had to finish the loaf. It would have been damaging evidence. Another couple of bites, and the last piece could go into the bin.

Lola could evacuate any thoughts that disturbed her. She blinked them out of her head. Three blinks and all bothering thoughts vanished. The only problem was that most of anything else that was in Lola's head was also blinked out.

Lola had difficulty feeling the life in her. She often breathed herself dead. Her breathing would become slow and shallow. She could sit in one spot for hours. She could be with her children, she could be in the middle of a group of people and appear enchanted by the conversation, but she was somewhere else, and she was dead. If she was not as dead as all the dead, then she was almost as dead.

Mr Lipnowski, who often ate at the Scheherezade, came up to Lola. 'I did see the wonderful drawing Garth did do in the newspaper. Such a beautiful drawing. You can see the suffering of the whole world in the eyes. The way he drawed those eyes. Beautiful.'

'What about my article?' said Lola.

'Too short,' said Mr Lipnowski. 'Too short, and I didn't learn anything from it.'

Lola was in a good mood. Her analyst had told her that unless she worked at this analysis she would have to leave. The news had shocked her. She felt more alive than she had for weeks. She smiled at Mr Lipnowski.

She remembered a conversation she had had with Mr Lipnowski last summer. Her book of poetry about life in a concentration camp had just come out. Mrs Frydman from the bookshop around the corner didn't want to order any copies until she saw whether there was a demand for the book.

'I was in Auschwitz,' she said, 'so, do I write poems?'

Mr Lipnowski had said to Lola, 'I told Mrs Frydman she should be selling gutkes, not books.'

Gutkes, Lola had explained to Garth, were underpants.

Halfway through her analysis, Lola saw that this apparent harshness, this callousness, this bluntness, was an endearing directness, a brisk and efficient communication. They all spoke like that. Mr Lipnowski, Mrs Frydman, Mr and Mrs Bensky. 'This is right. This is wrong. This is bad. This is terrible. This is no good. This is how I see things. This is this.' They all knew.

Their children had trouble knowing whether this was this, or this was not this. Lola's friend Ben, whose father had fought with the partisans in Poland and now owned Sunsoaked Swimwear Industries, belonged to the Shiva Yoga Centre. Every morning, between 5 and 6, Ben danced to Indian chants. From 6 to 7 he meditated. For the rest of the day he worked on his idea for a contemporary theatre production of the Ramayana Ballet.

Ben smiled at everything. In recent years, as he had climbed the executive rungs of the ashram, he had become more interested in his Jewishness. He now interspersed his 'oms' with 'oys'.

And then there was Morris Lubofsky. Lola found it hard to believe that Morris was the offspring of Rivka Lubofsky. Orphaned at thirteen by the Nazis, Rivka had spent the war hiding in the forests of Poland. Lola was mesmerized by Rivka's beauty. Rivka had fiery, dark-red hair and enormous, seductive and inviting eyes. She spoke six languages. And she laughed. She laughed with her whole body.

Rivka completed her Master of Laws degree in the same year that Morris dropped out of dentistry to edit the *Teenybopper*.

One hour after he had arrived at his parents' place, and twenty minutes after he had finished his regular Sunday lunch with them, Morris Lubofsky, forty years old and thrice divorced, lay on the couch in his parents' lounge-room. His stomach heaved gently and he slept.

Last Sunday at lunch Mr Lubofsky had given Morris the brochure for a new Jaguar Sovereign.

'Delivery will be in December. Happy Birthday.'

'Oh. Great. Thank you,' said Morris, and he went to the couch and slept.

Lola had observed this impossible-to-stay-awake-in-front-of-your-parents disease. She had discussed it with Morris's Catholic first wife, who was infuriated and bewildered by it. Lola had seen it in herself.

Lola never looked excited or enthusiastic in front of Mr or Mrs Bensky. She rarely expressed surprise, and never showed any joy, light-heartedness or happiness in their presence. She appeared to have no sense of humour. She never laughed when she was with them.

Occasionally they had caught her laughing with a friend.

Lola once saw Mr Bensky look at her with great surprise when she exploded with laughter while telling her friend Margaret-Anne the story of how she had met Dean Robertson, who was a top political journalist and a former colleague of Lola's. Lola's son was five at the time, and going through a stage of adding 'l' to every word. He said bookl, smokel, dogl, catl. Dean Robertson had asked Lola what she was doing now. 'I'm just a housewifel,' she had answered. Dean Robertson had fled with a nauseous grimace of farewell.

Lola looked at a photograph of Garth that she carried around in her wallet. He didn't look Jewish. He looked too happy.

Even the language tapes that Lola and Garth were learning Yiddish from were not too cheerful. Each phrase was stated slowly and then repeated. The conversation on the subject of 'How Are You?' went like this:

How are you?
Fine, thank you.
Not bad.
So so.
I don't feel well.
What's wrong with him?
He has a headache.
She doesn't feel well.
What's the matter with her?
She has a toothache.
We are ill.
What's wrong with you?
We have stomach aches.
I don't feel well.
What's wrong with you?
My feet hurt.
My parents aren't well.
What's wrong with them?
They have heartaches from their children.
My head hurts.

Her back hurts.
His hands hurt.
Your bones hurt.
Our feet hurt.
Their feet hurt.

By the time she was twenty, Lola knew no Jews. She worked as a rock journalist. Her three close girlfriends were pale, tall and angular, and, she realized on reflection, all prone to constipation.

She fell in love with blond, blue-eyed men whose fathers were president of the golf club and whose mothers had been the school hockey captain. Jewish boys looked awful to Lola. They looked spoilt and soft and unmanly. They looked frightened of their mothers, frightened of their fathers. 'Jewish boys have still got their mother's breast-milk on their faces,' said Margaret-Anne.

When Lola and Johnny Rosenberg were eighteen, he had driven his father's Vauxhall into the back of another car. Lola had had several stitches in her knees and Johnny Rosenberg had broken his nose. He sat in the Royal Melbourne Hospital and wept. 'How can I ring up my parents? The shock will kill them.'

Killing their parents was something that most Jewish children felt they had the power to do. Common fragments of conversation among the children were: 'This is going to kill my mother.' 'I can't tell my mother, it would kill her.' 'I couldn't do that, my father might die.' 'I can't leave my wife, it would kill my parents.'

Lola was no exception. Rather than kill her parents, Lola lied about everything. She lied about her non-Jewish boyfriend. The Benskys were perfectly happy to see Lola going steady with Angus Nankin, a 'Scottish Jew'. Mr and Mrs Nankin played along. Mr Nankin wore a yarmulka at dinner, and on Yom Kippur they all went to synagogue together. Mrs Bensky explained to her friends that these

Anglo-Jews could never speak Yiddish. The Benskys thought it was a shame when Lola and Angus broke up.

Lola lied about being a virgin, she lied about what she ate, she lied about studying at the Sorbonne. After she finished high school, Lola had begged the Benskys to send her to Paris to do a Diploma of Languages at the Sorbonne. Lola spent two days at the Sorbonne. She felt lonely, lost, and unable to be understood. She flew to London, bought an old London taxi cab and drove around Europe for six months. She drove through Italy, Spain, France, Germany, Austria, Switzerland. She put the car on a ferry in Naples and went to Israel, where she visited her cousin on a kibbutz in the Negev. A Parisian student rerouted Lola's mail, and everybody was happy. Mr and Mrs Bensky still boasted about Lola's gift for languages, and how she topped her class at the Sorbonne. Lola knew that people didn't die of lies.

She did fear her parents' deaths though, and did feel that whenever and however they died, it would be her fault.

She sympathized with Morris Lubofsky. When people talked about what a rich man he would be one day, Morris always said 'I hope I die before my parents.' Lola knew exactly what he meant.

'You will cry on my grave but it will be too late,' Mrs Bensky said to Lola over and over again. What if she didn't even cry then? Lola used to wonder.

Now she wondered how she could have been so cruel. So indifferent. How could she have been so unsympathetic, so uninterested in what Mrs Bensky had been through?

When Lola began to think about Mrs Bensky's life, she couldn't understand why, after the war, Mrs Bensky had still wanted to live, or why she had wanted to have children. Lola felt that she herself would have given up. She had given up many times. She had felt that nothing was worth while. This feeling, Lola now recognized, was a sad luxury. That nothing-really-interests-me, everything-is-so-tedious syndrome. It was usually accompanied by the my-parents-have-ruined-my-life philosophy, and had as a postscript, and-they-can-pay-for-it.

Lola folded her copy of the *Jewish News*. She had had a slice of apple cake, even though this was the first day of her new diet. She paid for her coffee and cake. She waved goodbye to Tivele. She smiled at Mr Rosenberg and Mr Schwarz, who were sitting at the front table, and she went home.

If You Live Long Enough

'Mmm, Elizabeth is so beautiful.' Morris Lubofsky was talking about his twenty-five-year-old girlfriend. 'She's got such strong limbs. You should see her close up. I mean really close up. People look very different really close up.'

Lola Bensky and Morris Lubofsky were walking along Lygon Street. Morris continued his conversation enthusiastically. 'You know, she's a really fabulous singer. There's no-one in the country who can sing like her.' Lola said nothing.

Sometimes Lola had to remind herself that she was very fond of Morris. She liked his sense of humour, and his dogged loyalty. When Morris held these conversations about his girlfriend, Lola didn't have to look interested. Morris was entertaining himself. He didn't notice Lola's lack of response.

Morris usually rang Lola several times a week. He rang to say how beautiful Elizabeth was, or how brilliantly her photography was progressing. Sometimes he wanted to relate what he had bought for his house, or what he intended to buy. Morris lived in a 20,000-square-foot converted dairy in Williamstown.

'She says I'm a fabulous lover,' Morris said. Lola didn't know what to say. They went on walking. 'We spent all yesterday in bed, and I'm meeting her for a production conference at home this afternoon.'

Morris was emerging. He was re-entering the world. He had been a dilettante. An editor of unsaleable newspapers. Morris had founded the *Teenybopper* and the underground 1970s weekly *The Joint*. His last venture had been the *Vegetarian Monthly*.

Now, with an initial capital investment of $500,000 provided by his father, Morris had formed an advertising agency. He specialized in television jingles.

Even when he had worked on the *Teenybopper*, whose circulation had peaked at five hundred a week, Morris was always on the phone. Now that he was in advertising, he had installed a telephone with eight lines, a fax machine and four computers. Whenever you rang Morris Lubofsky, whether it was 6 a.m. or 11 p.m., he was always on another call. 'Hello, hold on, I'm on another line,' he would say.

When Lola rang him up, she made sure that she had a book to read or some work to do while she waited for Morris to finish his other calls.

Now, listening to Morris, Lola realized what it was that she couldn't bear about him. He was always absorbed in himself. This was too close to what Lola was fighting in herself. It was that self-centred part of her that she knew she had to get rid of.

Why was it, Lola wondered, that a generation of robust, earthy, vigorous parents had produced cool cats like Morris, or comatose hypochondriacs like Fay Farber or Susan Wiener, or repressed depressives like Ben Hertz, who meditated and ommed all day?

Their parents had been in concentration camps, labour camps, ghettos. They'd survived for years during the war in bunkers, in forests and in haystacks.

They came to Australia damaged and penniless. But they were also resilient. They came here with gratitude, and spirit, and optimism, and a readiness to begin again. They built new lives. And they had children.

They wanted only the best for their children, and they

gave them everything. 'I am doing everything for the children. I want nothing for myself,' Renia Bensky used to say to Lola from the time Lola was a small child.

Lola never believed her. Renia would come home from the city with a new cocktail dress. 'Look, Lola, Mr Gross did give me this dress for almost nothing. It was a sample, and I am lucky that I am, of course, a perfect SSW, and it fitted me perfectly.'

There was always something for Lola in this shopping. 'Lola darling,' Mrs Bensky would say, 'I did buy you some new singlets. Pure cotton. Imported from England. They were so expensive. It is something shocking how much they cost.' Lola added them to her pile of pure cotton singlets and underpants.

Morris was still talking. They had walked to the Café Roma, where they were to meet Garth for lunch. Garth was late. After half an hour, Morris and Lola began lunch without him.

'My mother's chosen this fabulous lounge suite for me,' said Morris. 'It's grey leather, art deco. It's got three couches and two armchairs,' he said. He took another mouthful of spinach lasagne and continued talking. 'This new diet I'm on is really good. I went off it last week and gained half a stone, but as I'd lost one and a half stone, that's still a net loss of one stone. It's just a matter of what foods you eat with what. Like, you never mix carbohydrate and protein.'

Lola yawned. Morris Lubofsky was the centre of his world. And his world was the best world. His chiropractor was the best chiropractor. The coffee at Café Nero, next to his house, was better than the coffee at the café next to your house. In fact, according to Morris Lubofsky, the coffee at Café Nero was the best coffee in Melbourne. His barrister was the best barrister in Australia, and his proctologist was the best proctologist in the world. When Morris Lubofsky was a vegetarian, meat was poison. Now that he was a carnivore, raw eye fillets of beef minced with seaweed and soy sauce could save your life.

Morris Lubofsky was now talking about his haemorrhoids. 'You know,' he said, 'haemorrhoids are often a sign of bowel cancer. I'm getting rid of mine. Nowadays they can just tie an elastic band around them, and snap them off. Like crutching sheep.' Lola felt worn out. Not talking about herself had exhausted her.

Garth finally arrived. Lola was overjoyed to see him. They had been married for ten years now, and Lola still felt a soaring happiness when she saw him. Garth kissed Lola for just a moment too long for Morris. Morris coughed uncomfortably. 'OK, break it up, boys,' he said.

Garth was luminous, Lola thought. His smile lifted him out of the ranks of mortal men. She was besotted by him. And he was devoted to her. He quietened her fears and her nervousnesses. He never panicked. He relished the present, and looked forward to the future.

Lola was mesmerized by people who made long-term plans. How could anybody be certain of what could happen in the future?

Often, in the morning, Lola woke before Garth. She would lie in bed and look at him. He always looked as peaceful as a baby. As contented as a cat. Comfortable with himself. This morning, he had had one leg stretched out on top of the doona, and half a buttock exposed.

Lola slept with the doona wound around her. She slept curled in a ball. She hugged herself in her sleep.

'Freedom was never something you allowed yourself,' her first analyst had written, in a letter he had sent her years after she had left him. Lola didn't quite understand what he meant, but she had been pleased with the sympathetic tone.

Renia and Josl Bensky had been appalled when Lola left Rodney for Garth. Now, things were different. Josl proudly told anyone who would listen that he 'wouldn't exchange Garth for twenty Jews'. Garth could always gauge his rating

with Josl. On a really good day, Josl wouldn't swap him for fifty Jews.

Garth had a good sense of humour. He made even Renia laugh. He introduced a levity to the meals that they shared together. Garth loved Renia and Josl Bensky. He wasn't in awe of them or afraid of them. He wasn't shackled by the notion that anything he said could kill them. He teased them. He confided in them. He was generous to them. The relationship between the Benskys and Lola began to have a fluidity and a freedom and ease that they had not experienced before.

Morris, Lola and Garth shared a Zuppa Inglese and a crème caramel. Morris had said that he wouldn't have any dessert. He had then eaten most of the custard from the Zuppa Inglese, and now he was demolishing the crème caramel. 'Garth, did I tell you about my diet?' he asked.

Jews are all diet experts, Lola thought. No Jews overlooked the importance of weight loss. Last week, Lola had been at Izzy Staub's funeral. It was a very moving service. Izzy had been a much-loved man, and many people among the mourners were weeping. After the funeral, Lola waited in line to offer her condolences to Izzy's daughters, Eva and Irena. Eva and Irena were both distraught. Irena's eyes were swollen and red. She looked up as Lola went to speak to her. 'Look, Eva, look at how much weight Lola has lost. How did you do it?' Lola felt cheered by the thought that, even in the middle of death, weight loss was important. She made herself laugh, driving home from the cemetery, with the thought that at a Jewish funeral weight loss was a grave issue.

Morris was still talking about his diet. Lola could see that Garth was cross-eyed with boredom. Garth had never been on a diet. Morris was communicating with great intensity. He was giving Garth the details of how much weight he had gained and how much he had lost.

The obsession with food must be genetically built into Jews, Lola thought. Josl Bensky had been thirty-two when he came to Australia after the war. The few details of the first thirty-two years of her father's life that her father talked to her about were to do with food.

Once or twice a year, Josl would reminisce about the ham he used to eat. 'Oy,' he would say. 'Oy, was that a special good ham they made in Poland! I used to go to the Grand Hotel in Lodz. They made the best ham. It was almost sweet tasting. My father would have killed me if he had known that I was eating ham.'

Lola's earliest memories were of herself at Bialik kindergarten. She remembered hoping that she would have time to fit in a second helping of chocolate custard before her mother came to pick her up.

Lola's most humiliating memories were also to do with food. While the rest of the ten-year-olds at the Marilyn Brown School of Dancing were performing the final dress rehearsal of 'Fella With An Umbrella', Lola was in the dressing room, eating Shirley Berry's lamington.

When Mrs Brown confronted the class and said sternly, 'OK, who has stolen Shirley Berry's lamington slice?' Lola kept quiet. She hoped that she didn't have any crumbs on her face.

Later, feeling uncomfortable, Lola comforted Shirley Berry. They both agreed that the thief was probably Cheryl Buchanan.

The other humiliating episode Lola almost couldn't bear to recall. It was when she'd stolen Dr Bender's bananas. The Bender family and the Bensky family had gone away together for a week to Rosebud. Lola had been seven. Dr Bender was their dentist. She was a quiet, thin and intense woman. Dr Bender and her husband and daughter had been in Bergen-Belsen for six months. When they were liberated, Mr Bender had to spend six months in hospital before he could eat without vomiting.

Dr Bender couldn't work legally as a dentist. The Australian government didn't recognize her Polish qualifications. She was halfway through a Bachelor of Dentistry at the University of Melbourne. She had, however, bought dental equipment and set up a practice at her home, working mostly at night. Most of her patients were newly arrived Jews. She was an excellent dentist, and she was cheap. Her practice thrived, and she could afford to keep studying.

This week in Rosebud was the Benders' first holiday in Australia. The two families kept their food in separate cupboards. This wasn't the way that Renia Bensky would have liked it. Renia would have preferred to pool the food, but she was gracious about Dr Bender's need for division and order.

On the first day, Lola took three bananas from the Benders' cupboard. 'Was there any particular reason why you ate our bananas?' Dr Bender asked Renia Bensky.

'What a stingy pig that Dr Bender is,' Renia said to Josl after the debacle had been sorted out. 'Here she is, an educated woman, and she acts like a pig. She has to count every piece of food, and she did accuse us like we were big criminals.' To Lola, Renia Bensky said 'Lola, you are a greedy pig.'

Lola couldn't look Dr Bender in the eye for years. She still felt uncomfortable when she thought about the bananas. When Lola was twenty-two, she had come across Dr Bender in Regent Street in London. They had had a cup of coffee together.

'You know, Lola, your house, when you were a child, was the tensest household I was ever in.' Lola didn't know what to do with this information. It shocked her. She wanted to ask a thousand questions. Why was it tense? In what way? What had Dr Bender observed about their lives? Dr Bender was the only adult who had ever suggested that the Benskys' home life was anything less than perfect.

Lola opened her mouth. But nothing came out. The questions stayed stuck in her.

Was Dr Bender talking about the noise in the house? There was always a lot of noise. There were doors opening and shutting, cupboards and drawers banging. There were kitchen noises and bathroom noises, and instructions and orders being shouted. Was that what Dr Bender had meant?

As a child, Lola had longed for silence. She envied those girlfriends whose parents took no notice of them. Lola felt that her parents were omnipresent. At the same time she felt that they were not there. She felt as though she couldn't get a grip on them. When she spoke, she felt that they didn't listen. They were distracted by something. Something larger. Something Lola couldn't share.

Morris Lubofsky ordered another crème caramel and three more coffees. 'Today is a write-off diet-wise, so I may as well pig myself,' he said. 'I'll go back on my diet tomorrow.'

Lola had a scientific theory about why all Jews were on a diet. She had told Garth about this theory last week, and he seemed to think that there could be some truth in it. She explained the theory to Morris.

'Morris, I think that you and I are genetically predisposed to putting on weight. See, I think that the Jews who survived concentration camps must have had very efficient metabolisms, and that's why they could survive on very little food. It stands to reason that the offspring of people with such slow metabolisms would have extremely slow metabolisms. That would explain why Garth can eat anything he likes and not put on weight, whereas you and I can eat hardly anything and get fat.'

'I think you've got something there,' said Morris Lubofsky.

Just then, Aviva Jacobsen walked into the Café Roma. Aviva was the child of concentration camp survivors. She was two or three stone overweight. Morris and Lola nodded at each other. Aviva was evidence of the validity of Lola's theory.

'Hi, guys, how are you?' Aviva said. 'I'm just between cases. I've got a sentencing at four o'clock, and I've got to get to the children's court before then, so I won't stop.' Aviva, a barrister, lived her life on the run. She was busy defending this murderer, that thief, this distraught father, that battered child. Lola often thought that Aviva was driven. When Aviva wasn't working, she went to the theatre, to the opera, to the cinema, to concerts, to art openings, to museums. She was always doing something. And always in a hurry. Lola found Aviva's ceaseless activity exhausting.

Aviva's sister, Fay, moved very slowly. Fay looked permanently tranquillized. She lived in Israel. Very few Israeli men were limp or insipid, but Fay Jacobsen had found one such Israeli and married him. They had four boisterous, unmanageable children, and their fifth child was due any day now. Fay and her husband were supported by her parents.

Lola had met Aviva and Fay's father last week. He told her he had just spoken to Fay. 'I did ask her', he said to Lola, 'how the economic situation in the country is. She said to me "I don't know, Dad. I don't have to work, Igal doesn't have to work. How do we know how the economy is?"' Mr Jacobsen looked both proud and troubled by his daughter's reply.

'You know, Lola,' Mr Jacobsen said, 'I had a dream when I came to Australia. My dream was to earn enough money so that my children would never have to worry about money. And I did it.' Mr Jacobsen looked bothered.

Morris Lubofsky was talking to Garth about his girlfriend Elizabeth's legs.

'She's got amazingly long legs,' he was saying.

'Morris,' said Lola, 'this relationship with Elizabeth will never last. Even if she marries you, she'll leave you in a few years. And then what will you do, look for wife number five when you're fifty? I saw the way Elizabeth looked at you when you had that hayfever attack. Her concern was efficient, not affectionate. Anyway, she's not Jewish, and she's too young for you.'

One of the nice things about Morris Lubofsky, Lola

thought later, was that he was very good-natured. 'At the moment I'm not really worried about how long the relationship will last,' Morris replied. 'I feel happy with Elizabeth. She's given me a confidence that I didn't have. She tells me I'm a fabulous lover, and that's been very good for me.'

Lola had someone in mind for Morris Lubofsky. It was her friend Roslyn. But Roslyn had a penchant for non-Jewish men. Her two husbands hadn't been Jewish. Lola was trying to show Roslyn the error of her ways. She was trying to persuade Roslyn that her next husband should be Jewish.

Roslyn and Morris would be a perfect match, thought Lola. Roslyn's mother had been in hiding, in Poland, during the war, and so had Morris's mother. Roslyn was very bright. She wouldn't take any crap from Morris if she was his wife. She'd put Morris on the right track, thought Lola.

A friend of Lola's had once said to her, 'Lola, you should marry someone who will make you more than you are, not someone who will make you less than you are.' Roslyn would make Morris Lubofsky more than he was. And Roslyn would no longer have to struggle. She had struggled all her life. She had worked full-time while getting her degrees. She had always had to support herself. Things would be easier for her as a member of the Lubofsky family. And Roslyn wouldn't exploit their wealth. Roslyn was a modest and independent girl.

Yes, Roslyn would make a perfect wife for Morris Lubofsky. Lola talked to Roslyn about the importance of marrying a Jewish husband. 'What about Garth?' said Roslyn. 'Garth is more Jewish than I am,' answered Lola. 'He knows more about Judaism than I do. Anyway, there are no other goys like Garth.'

Josl Bensky had been at Lola's house one day when Lola was talking to Roslyn. 'You have to stop running away from your Jewishness,' Lola had lectured Roslyn. 'You think that having a ham sandwich on Yom Kippur is the action of a mature person who has come to terms with themselves?' Lola asked Roslyn. 'You are Jewish,' Lola continued emphatically, 'and it is a very attractive part of you.'

Josl Bensky had been sitting between the two women. He looked amused. Was this the same girl, the same Lola, his daughter, who'd gone out with tow-truck drivers, who had dated a black African from Nigeria, who had been in love with drug-addicted rock-and-roll singers? Was this the same daughter who had rejected all her mother's match-making efforts? The same daughter who hadn't gone out with a Jewish boy since she was eighteen? Was this Lolala Bensky speaking?

'Lolala, my darling,' Josl Bensky said. 'There is an old Yiddish saying. It says, "If you live long enough, you see everything."'

Lola and Garth said goodbye to Morris on Lygon Street.

'Will you be here for coffee on Saturday morning?' asked Morris. Lola nodded. 'Good,' Morris said. 'See you then.'

Things Could Be Worse

Lola Bensky saw herself on the screen. There she was. She was the second guest on the right at Tsaytl and Motl's wedding in *Fiddler On The Roof*. It was her. The same hair, the same eyes, the same mouth, the same expression.

Now, the Lola on the screen was dancing. Look at her. Her skirts were whirling. She was turning this way and that way. Stepping to the right. Stepping to the left. Now she was clapping and dancing. She was dancing the hora. She was dancing the mitzvah-tensl. Now Lola Bensky could see that it wasn't her up on the screen in *Fiddler On The Roof*. Lola Bensky couldn't dance.

Lola had tried to dance. At sixteen, when her friends were jiving to Chubby Checker, Bobby Darren and Crash Craddock, Lola had tried to look like a carefree rock-and-roller. She had had the right rope petticoats, the right T-bar shoes, the right lipstick and the right hairstyle. But she had had the wrong expression. She looked anguished, embarrassed and uncomfortable. She had tried to keep smiling through 'Only The Lonely' and 'Boom Boom Baby', but her discomfort had dislodged her smile.

Lola had tried again in her early twenties, when dancing had become more creative. You could make up the movements or follow the go-go dancers. At Ziggy's discothèque, Lola had kept her eyes glued to the go-go dancers. Six go-go dancers danced in cages suspended from the ceiling. Lola often felt dizzy looking up at the dancers while she copied their arm and leg movements, but Lola had no talent for choreography. Her imagination didn't extend to dance steps. If she couldn't see the go-go dancers, she couldn't dance.

At twenty-three, Lola gave up dancing. She didn't dance again until she met Garth. Garth was a fabulous dancer. Lola clung to Garth as he turned and stepped and twisted around the dance floor. Garth held Lola close to him, and clutched her tightly. From this secure position, Lola Bensky could smile while she danced.

Lola had seen herself on the screen before. She had seen herself in old footage of the prisoners of Dachau being liberated by the American army. She knew that the young girl behind the barbed-wire fence in Dachau, in front of the ditch filled with dead bodies, was her.

Lola saw herself in photographs, too. She saw herself in photographs of street urchins in the Lodz ghetto. She saw herself in a photograph of a small girl sitting next to her dead mother in the ghetto. She saw herself in photographs of Jewish women smiling for the camera in displaced persons camps.

Lola also looked for relatives in these photographs. She searched through photographs, books and films for members of her family. She looked for the son that her parents had had before the war. She looked for her grandparents. She looked for her aunties and uncles and cousins.

In her handbag she kept a notebook with the names of her parents' parents and brothers and sisters. In this notebook, she also kept an index of the titles of the books on the Holocaust that she owned.

Lola hated the word Holocaust. It was too neatly wrapped into a parcel. There were no loose ends and no frayed edges. The Holocaust. It was a nice, compact abstraction. But what else could she say? The alternatives were so wordy. She could say the Nazi extermination of European Jewry.

She could say the destruction of the Jews by the Nazis. She could say Hitler's murder of six million Jews.

Lola had a library of over one thousand books on the Holocaust. She had read most of them. Lola had a good memory. She had always had a good memory. She could remember hundreds, if not thousands, of phone numbers. Conversations she had ten years ago, she could recall verbatim. Yet the facts and statistics of the Holocaust flew out of her head. She had to check and recheck the information. Was it in Bergen-Belsen that British troops had found over ten thousand unburied bodies? Was it there, in Bergen-Belsen, that five hundred inmates a day had died from typhoid and starvation in the week after liberation? Was it in Mathausen that the Nazis had murdered thirty thousand Jews in the last four months of the war? Lola had to check and recheck.

When she was thirty, Lola had begun to ask her parents about their experiences in the war. They had answered her questions, hesitantly at first, but they had answered. Lola had listened. She had listened quietly. She had taken notes. She had tape-recorded some of the conversations. She had videotaped a long interview with each of her parents. And still their stories blurred and wandered in her head.

Lola had been shocked to find that other Jews her age didn't know or couldn't remember what had happened to their parents during the war. Solomon Seitz, with his Oxford D.Phil, didn't know. Susan Shuster, a researcher for the Prime Minister, couldn't remember. Boris Kronhill, the physicist, had a vague idea. He told Lola that his mother had been in hiding in a convent and his father had been in a labour camp in Russia. Lola knew that Boris had it all wrong. Renia knew the Kronhills and had told Lola that Mrs Kronhill had been in Auschwitz and Mr Kronhill had been hidden in a haystack on a farm in Poland for two years.

Renia and Josl's friends thought that Lola, with all her questions and all her books, was crazy. 'What does she want to read books about concentration camps for?' said Genia Pekelman. 'Does she want to go crazy?'

Lola came out of the Adelphi theatre in Mordialloc. Mordialloc was a long way from Russia and the world of Tevya and Tsaytl and Motl.

Lola's mother had died nine months ago. Last night, Lola had been feeling out of kilter. She had seen in the *Herald* that *Fiddler On The Roof* was playing at the Adelphi, and she had decided that she needed to see it. This morning Lola had bought a packet of Fantales and a packet of Minties, and driven for an hour to Mordialloc to catch the early matinée session at the Adelphi.

There had been only five other people in the cavernous theatre. Lola thought that she and the four elderly women and one very old man must have been the only people in Melbourne who hadn't yet seen *Fiddler On The Roof*.

Now, outside the theatre, Lola felt a bit disconcerted. It was a bright, blue, hot day. Mordialloc looked prosperous. People were eating Chiko rolls and pies in the pizza shop next door to the Adelphi. Poor Tevya had been so poor that he had to carry his milk deliveries himself when his horse had become too old. Here everyone had a car and could afford a milkshake.

Lola bought a custard tart and drove back to Melbourne. On her way home she stopped at Texoform, the factory in which her father worked. Josl had been with Texoform for nine years. Josl's clothing company, Joren Fashions, like many small businesses, had closed down in the seventies. At first Josl had felt devastated. Now, he enjoyed his job at Texoform. He had his own office, and he was in charge of ordering the fabrics. Josl felt as though Texoform was his own company. He was overjoyed when he saved the firm money, and he worked hard to create a high morale and a sense of loyalty among the workers.

Josl was surprised to see his daughter, but then nothing

that Lola did really surprised Josl. For many years, Lola had been at odds with herself. At odds with him. At odds with his beloved Renia, who had died just when everything was looking promising. Renia had died when both of her daughters were happily married and her grandchildren were turning out to be everything she had hoped for in her own children.

Josl wiped away the tears that came when he thought about Renia. He still got up early every morning and tiptoed around the bedroom so that he wouldn't disturb her. And every morning he was jolted out of his quiet by the realization that Renia was no longer there. His darling Renia, the woman he had loved since he was twenty-two and she was sixteen, was dead.

Josl kissed Lola hello. He looked at her. Lola had changed. In her thirties Lola had changed, and all the things that Josl had loved in her as a small child had returned. He had loved her curiosity and her enthusiasm. And he had loved her laugh. When Lola was little she used to laugh and laugh. If something struck her as funny she would laugh with her whole body, with her whole being. She would be completely immersed in her laughter. It used to give Josl so much joy.

'Hi, Dad,' said Lola. 'The photo of Mum looks good on the wall. I like this new office. How are you, Dad?'

'I'm all right, Lola. I'm all right,' Josl answered.

'You know what I did today?' said Lola. 'I drove out to Mordialloc and went to the pictures. I haven't been able to work well lately, and I noticed that *Fiddler On The Roof* was playing, so I went and saw it.'

'You haven't seen *Fiddler On The Roof* before?' said Josl.

'No, I'd never seen it,' said Lola.

'You never saw *Fiddler On The Roof*? But everybody did see *Fiddler On The Roof*. What a picture! I loved *Fiddler On The Roof*. Topol was very good in the film, but that Hayes Gordon, who did play Tevya on the stage in Melbourne, he was terrific. He is not a Jew, yet he was one hundred per cent a Jew on the stage. Your Mum and I, we loved him. We saw him twice. I can't believe that until now you didn't see *Fiddler On The Roof*.'

'I'm glad that I went to see it,' said Lola. 'I loved it. Dad, I know it's not Wednesday, but will you have dinner with us tonight? I'm making a beautiful veal and beef klops with sauerkraut.'

'I don't want you to start again with the "can I eat with you" business,' said Josl. 'I told you, I'll come once a week and that's it. Klops with sauerkraut? Is it the same way that Mum made it?' Josl asked.

'It's exactly the way that Mum made klops and sauer-kraut,' said Lola.

'It is a little bit hard to say no to klops with sauerkraut. All right, all right, I will come, but don't put me in this position again. I'm not going to be a burden on you or anybody,' said Josl.

'Dad, you know that it makes us happy to see you,' said Lola.

'OK, Lola, OK. I will come but I won't stay long. I want to have an early night. I didn't sleep so well last night. I started thinking, and I couldn't fall asleep. It's no good to think too much. It can get you so mixed up. I started to feel crazy. First I was thinking about Mum. She did everything right. She was slim, she didn't smoke, she did do exercise, and still she died. She was young. Sixty-three is not old today. Then I started to think about the past, and that maybe what happened to Mum in Auschwitz was what did give her the cancer. After a few hours thinking like this you can think you are crazy. It's better not to think too much,' said Josl.

'It's better not to think too much' was something Josl had said repeatedly since Lola was small. Lola had stopped thinking altogether when she was sixteen. Until then she had topped all her classes, played the piano well and won prizes for her French and German poetry recitations. At sixteen she failed two of her five final year high school subjects. The following year she had passed the two subjects that she had failed and failed the three that she had passed. The third time, to everyone's relief, she passed all five subjects.

Lola had drifted through the next ten years. She became a journalist. She became a wife. She became a mother. She seemed like a good journalist, a good wife and a good mother. But Lola was crooked. She was skewwhiff. She was at an odd angle. And no-one noticed.

Arrows of anger and shafts of self-pity pitted her thoughts. Fear ruptured her nights. Fantasies and dreams were intertwined with her daily life. She thought she was Renia and Josl. She thought she had been in the ghetto. She thought she had been in Auschwitz too.

Lola had always been plump. But from the age of sixteen, she grew, slowly and steadily, until she was huge. She grew a cocoon around herself. And in this unoccupied territory, this haven, this no man's land, Lola, a bit breathless and tired, spent her youth.

Lola didn't start thinking again until she was twenty-six and went to see a psychoanalyst about her weight problem.

'What sort of answer is that to a weight problem?' Renia had said when Lola asked her to look after Julian while she went to the analyst. 'Is this a solution to being fat? To go to a psychiatrist? What sort of a solution is that?' said Renia.

'Lola is going to see an analyst about losing weight?' said Ada Small. 'Why doesn't she go to Weight Watchers? Whoever heard of somebody going to see a doctor for mad people, for meshuganas, when she just wants to lose some weight? It's crazy.'

'What about a hypnotist?' suggested Genia.

'What about Limmits biscuits, or the egg-and-grapefruit diet?' said Renia to Lola. 'I have heard some very good reports about that egg-and-grapefruit diet. You can have as many boiled eggs as you like, as long as you eat half a grapefruit first. Lola, what did we do to deserve the shame of a daughter who goes to see a psychiatrist?'

'You think too much and you don't do enough dieting,' Josl had said. 'Anyway,' he had continued, 'I have heard some not very good things about this Herr Professor, this expensive doctor psychiatrist. I heard he got divorced from a very nice woman. I heard that he is the meshugana, not the patients that he treats. The worry about this is making your mother sick. Her daughter is going to see a lunatic doctor. She needs this like a hole in the head.'

Lola had decided that it hadn't been a good idea to ask Renia to babysit Julian. She came to an arrangement with her friend Margaret-Anne. Margaret-Anne would look after Julian twice a week while Lola went to her analyst, and Lola would babysit Margaret-Anne's Jonathan while Margaret-Anne was at meditation classes.

Lola had always had close women friends. She spoke to them every day. She had cooked food for their husbands when her friends were in hospital having children. She had scoured the real-estate pages of the newspapers and visited properties with them when they were buying houses. Her friends were her substitutes for sisters.

Although she had tried to see little Jonathan as family, his shit stank and she couldn't understand him. After six months Lola had hired a babysitter for Julian.

Lola had tried other ways of creating a large family. She had arranged book clubs, film clubs and card nights. She had tried to organize a communal housing project. Lola had wanted her friends to sell their houses and build new houses on a large block of land that had come up for sale in Melbourne. This land was fifteen minutes from the city, and had a thousand feet of river frontage. Lola had envisaged a beautiful environment where they could all still have their privacy, but they would be able to develop deeper friendships with each other. They would be able to share some of the domestic drudgeries of having young children, and they would also be able to afford luxuries such as a swimming pool and a tennis court.

Lola had cajoled, arranged, organized, pressed and begged her friends. The proposed project had divided the group. The book and film clubs and the card nights came to an end.

Charlie Goldstein, Lola's old school friend, had asked Lola why this large group of friends no longer spoke to each other.

Lola had replied, 'We were split up by my proposal that we become closer.'

This was a liberated era. Charlie Goldstein, still wide-eyed, had told his partner Hyram that, although Lola Bensky didn't look the type, she had told him, and he had heard it with his own ears, that she had tried to organize a wife-swapping commune.

The news had spread through Melbourne. Mrs Goldstein, Charlie's mother, had rung Renia Bensky.

'Renia darling,' she had said, 'I hear you are having a bit of trouble with Lola. Just be strong, Renia. Like my dear departed mother used to say, "Small children small worries, big children big worries."'

'That idiot Mrs Goldstein rang me today,' Renia had said to Josl that evening. 'She rang to let me know that she knows how fat Lola is. "Be strong, Renia," she said. With friends like Mrs Goldstein, who needs enemies?'

'Renia darling,' said Josl, after he had agreed that Mrs Goldstein was a philistine, a peasant and an idiot, 'Renia darling, I think that Lola is losing a bit of weight. Do you think there is a chance that that lunatic doctor is doing her some good?'

'Who knows what would do Lola good?' said Renia. 'I think I will make her a dish of zucchinis and tomatoes. I got the recipe from Nusia who got it from Mrs Braunstein who is going to Weight Watchers.'

Lola was just leaving Josl's office when he called her back. 'Lola, I nearly forgot. I bought some dog food for you. Pal dog food. The brand Mum always bought. It was on special, so I bought two boxes. I'll put them in the boot for you.'

Lola had inherited her mother's dogs. Lola, who had no interest in dogs or cats, was now the owner of Cleo, Benny and Blacky.

Lola was sure that Renia had been the only Jew in Melbourne to own three dogs. Cleo, Benny and Blacky had all been strays. They had attached themselves to Renia, who couldn't bear to see homeless or hungry animals.

Josl put the boxes of dog food in the car. 'Thanks, Dad,' said Lola. 'I'll see you tonight.'

Lola drove towards St Kilda. She felt better. Seeing *Fiddler On The Roof* had cheered her up, and she was happy that Josl was coming for dinner. She wished that her mother wasn't dead. Why did her mother have to die? In the last few years she and her mother had been getting on so well. Lola's throat constricted with choked tears. She hadn't been able to cry for her mother since the funeral.

On St Kilda Road, Lola started to think about how good her life was. She loved Garth, and he loved her. The kids had turned out well. Julian was a medical student.

'My son is two-thirds of a doctor,' Lola boasted. When Renia was in hospital dying, Renia had told every nurse, every intern, every orderly and every specialist that her grandson was a medical student. It had made Lola weep. It had also consoled her. At least she had given Renia a grandson who had given her a lot of pleasure.

Even when he had been a small boy, Julian had been able to make Renia happy. When Renia was with Julian all her anger evaporated and all her anguish vanished. Renia had played with Julian, fed him, walked with him, talked with him. Lola had felt that little Julian had healed and soothed Renia in a way that her own children had never been able to.

When Julian was older, Renia collected his prizes and certificates. The two of them went for long walks along the beach together. Sometimes, on these walks, people had complimented Renia on her handsome son, and she had glowed. 'Julian is as good at maths as I was,' Renia used to say to Lola. Lola had always been hopeless at maths.

Lola arrived at Polonsky's kosher butcher shop. Though her parents had never been Orthodox, Lola bought kosher meat. Josl used to laugh at her. 'The kosher meat is twice the price and it doesn't taste any different,' he would say. Lola knew it was irrational, but she felt that the veal and beef were better for having been blessed.

Mrs Kopper was inside Polonsky's.

'Hello, Lola,' she said, 'and how's things? How are you keeping? Are you and your sister still broygis with each other? It's a shocking thing that two sisters should not speak to each other. Thank God your poor dear mother, God rest her soul, didn't see this. It is shocking. I saw your father the other day and he told me how upset he was about you two girls. I tell you, Lola, there was a tear in his eyes. I told him, I said to him, "Josl, things could be worse." And it is true. To make your father feel better I reminded him about the old Sholem Aleichem story. You know, the story about the bags of worries. You don't know this story? You didn't hear about it? Well, I will tell you, Lola.

'There was a village where many people had troubles. They came to the rabbi and said "Rabbi, why do I have to have so much trouble? My neighbour doesn't have such troubles. Why was I chosen to have this trouble?" The rabbi heard these complaints many times. One day the rabbi said that everyone who had troubles should put their troubles in a bag, and bring the bag to the market place. The people of the village did this. Then the rabbi said that everyone should choose someone else's bag to take home. When the people got home and saw what was in the bag of troubles that they had chosen, they said, "Oh God, please give me my own troubles back. My own troubles were not so bad." The next day everyone returned to the market place to get back his own bag of troubles.'

'Excuse me,' said Mrs Singer. 'I know that you are telling this story, Mrs Kopper, but it is important to tell it right. I don't think that Sholem Aleichem said that many people in the village had troubles, just a few people.'

'All right, all right, Mrs Singer,' said Mrs Kopper. 'What does it matter? That is not so important. What is important is what I was trying to tell Lola. And that is that things can always be worse.'

'I can tell you straight away about two sisters who are worse,' said Mrs Singer. 'My neighbour has got three nieces. The two younger girls hate the oldest girl. I hear that she is not such a nice person but that is another story. My neighbour's brother, the girls' father, died last month. The younger girls told their older sister, who lives in Canberra, that the funeral was at eleven o'clock. When the older girl arrived at the cemetery, the funeral was finished, because the funeral was really at ten o'clock. And of course, everybody was talking about how shocking it was that the older daughter didn't come to her father's funeral.'

Lola knew that things could always be worse. It was something that she had always been sure of. Mr Polonsky gave Lola her minced veal and beef.

'Well, Lola,' he said, 'you are a big star now. A famous person. I see your photograph in the *Jewish News* every week. When you left here last time, Mrs Leber asked me if that was Lola Bensky the writer. "Yes, Mrs Leber," I said. "Lola Bensky always buys her meat and chickens here."'

Lola drove home. At home she prepared the klops mixture. This was her mother's recipe. Two eggs, two chopped onions, two grated cloves of garlic, two tablespoons of breadcrumbs, two teaspoons of salt and half a teaspoon of pepper for every kilo of meat. It made a delicious meatloaf.

Lola kneaded and kneaded, listening to the soft sound of the meat on her fingers. The meat and onions and eggs and garlic and breadcrumbs blended into a smooth universe.

Maybe one day she would be able to patch things up with her sister, Lola thought. Although it wasn't really a patching job, more like a total overhaul. She put the klops into the oven.

Technical Trouble

The Prime Minister had finished his speech. Everybody was clapping. There were five hundred people here, in the forecourt of Parliament House. The Prime Minister had planted a tree in honour of Raoul Wallenberg, the Swedish diplomat who had saved tens of thousands of Jews from the Nazis.

Lola Bensky stepped up onto the podium to read her poem about Raoul Wallenberg. Lola was nervous. She was so nervous that her hands and legs shook almost as though they had been choreographed.

Lola cleared her throat away from the microphone. She began to read. The words came out of her mouth and dissolved in the hovering humidity. The microphone was not working.

There were mutterings and stirrings from the crowd.

'The microphone has broken,' said Mr Rosen.

'Oy, it's broken,' said Mr Berg.

'The microphone has broken down,' said Mrs Roth.

'It's not working,' said Mrs Fink.

'That microphone is not working,' said Mr Mendelson.

No-one moved.

The Prime Minister got back up onto the podium. He tried to fix the microphone. He turned and twisted the knob at the base of the microphone.

'It's broken,' said Abe Rothberg.

'Yes, it's broken,' said Sadie Levin.

The Prime Minister tried again. He found a switch at the side of the microphone and switched it on and off. But nothing happened.

'It's definitely broken,' said Mrs Dunov.

'It's broken,' said Mr Fishman.

'You'll have to shout,' the Prime Minister said to Lola.

How could Jews be so clever, and so inept? thought Lola. Jews could feed three thousand people without a hitch, but it was beyond them to find one microphone in working order for a special occasion.

Lola looked at the crowd. There was Sol Apelbaum, managing director of Consolidated Metal Industries. Consolidated Metal Industries had offices in Hong Kong and Singapore. Next to him were Wolf Nathanson of Proctor Properties and Sam Baume, head of the Sweet Evelyn chain of retail stores. How, wondered Lola, had they managed to build such successful businesses without knowing how to fix a microphone?

In the past year Lola had read her poetry at many Jewish functions. The microphone had not worked once. Josl had explained to her that microphones were not what Jews knew about.

'It's not their field,' he had said.

The crowd was becoming more agitated. People shook their heads and said 'It's not working.' Lola looked feebly at the Prime Minister. 'I think you'd better shout,' he said again.

Lola shouted the sad poem about Raoul Wallenberg.

Four hours later, the dinner after the tree-planting ceremony was progressing well. The guests had already had hors d'oeuvres, soup and an entrée. The waiters were serving the main course. The dessert, the cakes and the coffee were yet to come.

Lola was enjoying herself. There she was, sitting among five hundred Jews, and she was enjoying herself.

Lola looked around the room. The atmosphere was buoyant and celebratory. Most of the guests had come from Melbourne and Sydney. Lola could see the energy of the people, the vitality, the good humour, the warmth.

She could see what she had prevented herself from seeing for years: she could see that she was at home here. This was a familiar world. She understood the language, the mannerisms, the meanings and the intentions.

A woman in her sixties came up to Lola. 'Lola, you don't remember me, but I am Mrs Klineman. I used to know your parents when you were a young girl. I remember you well. What trouble you gave your parents, Lola! I remember when you were arrested for shoplifting. Your poor mother, it nearly killed her.'

Lola said that she would pass on Mrs Klineman's regards. Mrs Klineman was sitting at a table with Mr and Mrs Beir, Mr and Mrs Pilsen and Mr and Mrs Dorovitch. Mrs Klineman and Mrs Beir had been in Auschwitz together. Mrs Pilsen had hidden in the forests in Poland for four years during the war. Mr Beir had been in Dachau, and Mr Dorovitch had fought with the partisans.

When Lola thought about their pasts, and the pasts of many of the Jewish people in the room, she felt full of admiration for them. Mr and Mrs Klineman had canvassed for the release of Russian Jews for years. Mrs Beir was at every commemoration, every seminar and every book launching in the community. Mrs Dorovitch was on the Jewish Heritage Committee. They were tireless. They made speeches, delivered lectures, collected petitions, baked cakes, raised money and raised children. They were exemplary grandparents and were devoted to their grandchildren.

Somebody tapped Lola on the shoulder. It was Jack Zelman.

'I came up to Canberra for some business and heard you

were in town, so I thought I'd drop by and say hello,' said Jack Zelman.

Lola hadn't seen Jack for at least ten years. She'd heard bits and pieces about him from her mother. Lola had also heard news of Jack from Morris Lubofsky. Morris knew what everybody was doing.

Lola knew that Jack was forty-four and unmarried. She knew that he had had plenty of short-term relationships.

'Jack can only feel excited by women who are not his,' Morris Lubofsky had told her. 'It's true,' Morris had said. 'Jack always falls in love with someone else's wife. He stays in love with them until they look as if they might leave their husband for him, and then he falls out of love. He once told me that as soon as he imagines the woman as his wife, he becomes impotent.' Morris had felt that he should elaborate this point: 'Jack can't get an erection if he thinks that the woman might want to marry him. And this is a guy who is supposed to be one of the greatest shtoopers in town. Phew, what a problem.'

Lola hadn't been sure whether Morris Lubofsky had been ironic or envious. She hadn't had time to ask him, because Morris's real area of interest was himself, and he had already been derailed for too long on the subject of Jack Zelman.

Morris had wanted to tell Lola about his new shoes. 'I had to get these new sports shoes,' he had said earnestly. 'I was falling over, walking in ordinary shoes. I can't wear ordinary shoes anyway. After three hours of wearing ordinary shoes, I'm so exhausted I have to go to bed. These new ones that I'm wearing have got three soles. The first sole hits the pavement, the second sole slides in along and absorbs the shock, and the third sole throws you into the next step.'

Lola thought that it must be a great help in life to have shoes that gave you a lift into the next step.

What a trio they made, Lola had thought. There she was,

a former bad girl, a reformed anti-Semite. And there was
Morris Lubofsky, divorced from his third wife, and still
buying himself toys. Cars, furniture, shoes. And Jack
Zelman, a property developer who could only fuck other
people's wives.

'You look very good. You look fabulous, actually, Lola,'
said Jack Zelman.

Lola started to laugh. One of her strongest memories of
her adolescence was of Jack Zelman.

'Lola,' he had said to her, 'if you went on a diet and lost
weight I'd take you out.' He had then gone on to explain to
Lola just how much weight he would like her to lose. He
wanted her to get down to the same size as Louise Samuels.

Louise Samuels was five foot nine and weighed eight
stone. Lola was told this by Jack's sister Mary. Lola was the
same height as Louise Samuels. Lola had often thought that
they must be the two tallest Jewish girls in Melbourne.
Unfortunately, Lola had calculated she was fifty per cent
heavier than Louise. She would have had to lose the
equivalent of half of Louise's body. Lola decided to give up
on Jack Zelman after that.

Jack looked embarrassed when she laughed. She wondered whether he was remembering too. They had a few
memories in common, she and Jack Zelman. She thought of
one of the many holidays they had had in Surfers Paradise.
The Benskys had been there with the whole company of
friends. Lola and Jack were sitting on the lawns of the
Chevron Hilton. It was early evening. They had known
each other since they were small children. They were
talking. Jack had stopped talking, and Lola was listening to
the quiet of the night. Lola loved silence. A cicada sent out
a long shriek, and suddenly Jack Zelman was kissing her.
He lay on top of her and pushed himself against her. She
could feel his hardness. It felt wonderful. Lola had an
orgasm.

'Oh God, what a mess,' was what Jack had said when he
spoke again. Lola had thought that the mess that he was

talking about must have been the intimacy they had shared. She thought that he had regretted the closeness. That he felt sullied.

Lola felt flushed, remembering that summer in Surfers Paradise. Jack was smiling at her. Lola introduced Jack to Garth. 'Garth, I'm so pleased to meet you. I hear from my mother all the time that you are the perfect son-in-law. Renia Bensky always said to my Mum that she wouldn't swap you for one hundred Jewish sons-in-law.' Garth laughed.

'Sit down and join us, Jack,' said Lola. She suddenly felt sorry for Jack Zelman. He didn't have a wife. He didn't have any children. Lola wondered why. Other people also wondered why. Jack Zelman was the bane of every Jewish matchmaker in Melbourne. He was their dream match. He was good-looking, educated and rich. He wasn't a faigele – on the contrary, he had a reputation for being a lion in bed. So why didn't he get married?

Lola knew that Jack had had a hard time at home as a kid. His parents, Mina and Joseph, had each been married to other people before the war. Mina's first husband, Tadek, Lola's mother had told her, had been the great love of Mina Zelman's life. Mina and Tadek had lived in the same street in Warsaw. Tadek was several years older than Mina. He used to take her on outings from the time that she was two and he was seven. At ten, Tadek had announced to his mother that he was going to marry Mina. When Mina was sixteen they were married. Their son, Henryk, was born the following year. Tadek and three-year-old Henryk died in Bergen-Belsen. When the British troops liberated Bergen-Belsen, they found Mina half-dead, on top of a pile of corpses.

Renia Bensky had once told Lola that she thought that Mina Zelman worked so tirelessly for charities in order to store up credit with the Almighty, so that when she died she would be reunited with Tadek and Henryk. This thought had given Lola the creeps.

Once her mother had said to her, 'Lola, Mina Zelman is giving away all of Joseph's money. She gives to this charity. She gives to that charity. The more Joseph earns, the more Mina gives. Joseph doesn't understand why Mina does so much giving, but he doesn't say anything. It keeps Mina happy, he thinks, and she doesn't ask him any questions about Pola Ganz. And, for the moment, he has still got plenty of money left.'

Lola didn't like Joseph Zelman. She thought that he was crude. She could understand Mina Zelman not being upset at the thought of Joseph having an affair with Pola Ganz. Lola thought that there was not a lot of tenderness or sensitivity in Joseph Zelman, so what difference would it make whether he was faithful or not? Pola Ganz probably wasn't getting anything that Mina Zelman needed, thought Lola.

Lola sometimes saw Joseph Zelman at her parents' place. He always wanted to tell her about his daughters, Mary and Susan. Lola hadn't seen the Zelman girls since they left Melbourne to live in Israel sixteen years ago. She had, however, seen endless photographs of them, their husbands and their children. Joseph always carried a walletful of photographs on him.

Joseph Zelman boasted about the sacrifices that his two daughters had made by choosing to live in Israel.

'It's not so easy to live in Israel,' he used to say. 'Susan and Mary could have a much more comfortable life in Melbourne, but they are committed to Israel, and Mina and I are very proud of their commitment.'

Lola thought that Susan and Mary were probably most committed to living away from their father. That way they all got on well together.

'It's a blessing to have such a close family,' Joseph would tell Lola.

The Zelmans always seemed to have just returned from another wonderful holiday with their daughters. 'We just had a marvellous holiday in Monte Carlo with the girls and their husbands and the children. We all get on so well together. We share the same interests. We went out every night. We had the most wonderful holiday. Yes, it's a blessing to have such a close family,' Joseph would say.

During the years when Lola was having trouble just being civil to her parents, let alone entertaining the thought of romping in Monte Carlo with them, Joseph Zelman's speeches used to make her hair stand on end.

Before the war, Joseph had been married to Mina's eldest sister, Malka. Malka and Mina were distantly related to Renia Bensky.

'Malka was a different sort of woman,' Renia used to say, mysteriously. 'She was a perfect match for Joseph. She was as hungry as him in every department. My aunty used to tell me that Malka could never keep her hands off Joseph.'

Mina was Malka's quiet, younger, taller, more awkward sister. Mina had met Joseph in Germany, hours after he had heard that Malka had perished in Dachau. Mina already knew that Tadek and Henryk were dead. She had watched them die.

Two months after they were married, Mina and Joseph arrived in Australia. They spent their first month in Australia at Bonegilla.

The air at Bonegilla was thick with the smell of boiling mutton. The smell lingered in people's clothes and in their hair. Mina felt as though her skin had absorbed the stench of the mutton. Mina avoided going to the huge pit that was used as a toilet as much as she could. She would wait until her bladder ached or she felt ill before she went to the toilet at Bonegilla.

Jack had been conceived at Bonegilla. The barracks at Bonegilla were segregated. Mina slept in the middle of a large, crowded women's dormitory. One afternoon, Joseph had wound two sheets around four chairs to create an area of privacy around the camp stretcher that was Mina's bed. He had then made love to Mina. Mina had wept with humiliation. When they had both emerged, Mrs Lovic and Mrs Platt and Mrs Antman, who slept in adjoining beds, were grinning.

One morning in Bonegilla, Mina thought that she could hardly remember what it was like to live in a normal home. For almost ten years she had gone from one set of barracks to another. From labour camp to concentration camp to displaced persons camp, and now to this 'Reception and Training Centre'.

Mina tried to remember the small apartment in Warsaw where she and Tadek had lived. Just as the memory was beginning to warm her, Mrs Lovic called her to come to what was called an English class. Very few people in Bonegilla spoke English. It was unnecessary. Living in the camp you could have picked up German, Polish, Italian, Latvian, Russian or Yiddish, but not English. The English class, that day in Bonegilla, was learning to sing 'Roaming in the Gloaming'. Mina still knew the words.

Joseph Zelman had had a good head for business. He had worked very hard, and now the Zelmans were very wealthy. Joseph had built large blocks of apartments all over Melbourne.

Joseph liked to live well. He went to the theatre, to the opera, to the cinema. Twice a year he flew to Switzerland to the Brechen-Bilt Clinic for a rest. He went to Germany for Alpine Air Inhalations at the Baden Rejuvenation Centre, and he went to Austria to have mud baths for his arthritis.

Joseph ate at the best restaurants and drank the best wines. Joseph dined at these restaurants with business colleagues, with friends, or with his son Jack.

Mina wouldn't eat in restaurants. She was suspicious of them. The few times she had eaten out, she had been ill afterwards.

When Joseph and Mina travelled, Mina ate raw vegetables, which she bought herself. Restaurant food was never clean enough for her. She had tried several times to explain this to Joseph. 'I don't want to eat food that has been touched by other people,' she used to say. 'I don't know who has touched the food, and if the cook has washed his hands, or if he has got a running nose or a bad cough.' Joseph was aggravated by Mina's attitude, but he never said anything.

Joseph felt that his own experiences during the war were so mild compared to Mina's that he could never criticize her. Joseph had been lucky. In 1939 he had been sent to a Russian labour camp. It may not have been a picnic, Joseph often thought, but when he compared it to Mina's wartime experiences he knew he had nothing to complain about.

In the centre of the sideboard in the Zelmans' dining room, in a large silver frame, was a small, yellowing, sepia photograph of a small boy. He had large, hooded eyes, chubby cheeks, and a sweet, bow-shaped mouth. The small boy looked just like Jack Zelman. He was Henryk Fischer, Mina's first son. The photograph was all Mina had from her life before the war.

When Jack was sixteen, he had told Lola that he didn't think he was Mina's real son. He thought that the boy in the photograph was Mina's real son. The boy in the photograph was never mentioned in the Zelman house. Jack didn't even know his name.

Jack had asked her if her parents had had any children before her. She had said no, even though she knew that her parents had had a stillborn son in the Lodz ghetto.

Lola didn't know why she had lied to Jack Zelman. Lola had woven so many of her own fantasies into the fabric of her parents' past that she could no longer remember what was true and what wasn't.

She had concocted a whole story about how her parents had been separated in Auschwitz, and had searched for each other after the war for six months. The story up to this point was true. From here, Lola added a scenario worthy of Cecil B. de Mille. Lola's story was that her mother and father had separately criss-crossed Europe by train looking for each other. They had often missed each other by seconds, and often passed each other on parallel train tracks going in opposite directions. After six months, neither had yet found out whether the other was alive. Finally, in Lola's story, her mother was asking a British soldier at a railway station in Germany if he had seen her husband.

'Yes I have, madam, and he's on that train,' the soldier had replied, pointing to a train that was just pulling out of the station. But all was not lost. The British soldier drove Lola's mother to the next station and she boarded the train. She walked through the carriages looking for her husband. Then she saw him, and fainted.

The Master of Ceremonies, Nathan Spatt, tapped the side of the lectern with a teacup.

'Ladies and gentlemen! Ladies and gentlemen! Quiet, please. I am going to call on Mr Sol Spigal, our president, who shall say a vote of thanks to the many people who have helped to make today a memorable day.'

'Jesus, look at all that saccharin,' said Jack Zelman. Lola looked around at the tables. There were two bottles of saccharin for every four place settings. An avalanche of saccharin was about to be dropped into five hundred cups of coffee.

'It's always puzzled me why Jews are so fixated by saccharin,' said Jack. 'They've just eaten apple strudel and ice-cream, and chocolates, and now they're making up for that by not putting sugar into their coffee. It's madness.'

'Yes, it's madness,' agreed Lola.

Mr Sol Spigal had twenty-five minutes of thank-yous. Everybody from Melbourne had to be thanked. Everybody from Sydney had to be thanked. And, of course, the local committee from Canberra had to be thanked. Each individual was thanked, and the audience applauded each thank-you.

The Master of Ceremonies returned.

'And now we have something very special to end our very special day. We have the honour to have with us tonight the wonderful poet Lola Bensky, and she is going to read her wonderful poem again for us.'

Lola stepped onto the platform. She was not so nervous now. She quietened herself for a minute. She took a deep breath, and began to read. There was an uproar in the hall.

'We can't hear. We can't hear,' echoed around the room.

'I think the microphone is not working,' said Nathan Spatt.

'I'll shout,' said Lola.